A Kill

Logan darted around his mount and drew both flintlocks.

Dega did the only thing he could think of; he spun and ran. He braced for a searing pain in his back but no shots boomed. Veering to avoid an oak, he spotted a thicket and without hesitation dived in, holding the bow at his side so it wouldn't become entangled. He went several steps and crouched.

"You're as dumb as a stump, boy."

Dega peered through the interwoven limbs and leaves. He hadn't moved fast enough. The white man was at the thicket, both guns leveled.

"Not that you'll live long enough for it to do you any good, but here's some advice. Never talk when you should kill. Never let yourself be distracted. Now come on out with your hands empty and I might let you live a bit."

WILDERNESS #61:
THE SCALP HUNTERS

David
Thompson

LEISURE BOOKS NEW YORK CITY

Dedicated to Judy, Joshua and Shane.
And to Beatrice Bean, with the most loving regard.

A LEISURE BOOK®

September 2009

Published by

Dorchester Publishing Co., Inc.
200 Madison Avenue
New York, NY 10016

ISBN 10: 0-8439-6261-5
ISBN 13: 978-0-8439-6261-1
E-ISBN: 978-1-4285-0735-7

The name "Leisure Books" and the stylized "L" with design are trademarks of Dorchester Publishing Co., Inc.

Printed in the United States of America.

10 9 8 7 6 5 4 3 2 1

Visit us online at www.dorchesterpub.com.

WILDERNESS #61:
THE SCALP HUNTERS

Chapter One

The four were young and eager for excitement. They liked to explore and roam where whim took them. Only one had counted coup. That didn't matter since they were careful to avoid their many enemies.

Short Bull in particular was tired of the same old haunts, the same old hunting grounds. He wanted to set eyes on country he had never seen before. So on the tenth night of their wandering, as he and his friends were hunkered around a crackling fire, he announced, "I am not ready to go back to our village. I want to see more of the prairie."

Plenty Elk grunted. "What is there to see but grass and more grass?"

Across the fire from them Wolf's Tooth said, "Were it up to you, we would not ride out of sight of our lodges."

Right Hand laughed. He had the best disposition. His mother liked to say that when he was born the sun lit his eyes and had burned bright ever since. "We have already come farther than any of our people have ever come. What is another five or six sleeps?"

They were young and they were Arapaho. The *Sariet-tethka*, some tribes called them; the Dog Eaters.

The Arapaho liked dog meat. To them it was delicious. To the other tribes it was the same as eating one's grandmother.

All four wore finely crafted buckskins and moccasins that each bore the personal stamp of the wearer. Right Hand's moccasins were white, to represent snow, with large blue triangles, the symbol for lakes. Wolf's Tooth's were mostly brown but had red squares that stood for buffalo guts. Plenty Elk's moccasins were brown, too, but with green rectangles to betoken the breath of life. Short Bull's had red markings that symbolized red crayfish.

Only Short Bull had an eagle feather in his hair. He was the one who had counted coup. "So we are agreed? We continue east?"

"I am for it," Right Hand said.

"And I," Wolf's Tooth declared.

Plenty Elk poked the fire with a stick and sparks rose into the air. "You are my friends. I will go where you go. But I am not as fond of grass as the rest of you. I am against this."

Right Hand grinned at the others, then said casually, "I have heard you are fond of antelope."

"Especially Small Antelope," Wolf's Tooth said, "even though she has two legs and not four."

Plenty Elk waited for their mirth to end before saying, "You envy me because she is as beautiful as a sunrise."

"Now she is," Wolf's Tooth agreed. "Have you seen her mother? That is how she will look in fifty winters."

"I would not shed tears if the Utes took your hair," Plenty Elk parried.

They were young, and they were best friends. Ever since they could remember they did everything together. They learned to ride together, to hunt together, to shoot bows together. Short Bull's father was a member of the Spear Society, warriors who vowed never to retreat in battle and taught them to throw a lance.

They had been to many places together. Up into the mountains where the snow stayed on the highest peaks even in the heat of summer. To the Black Hills, the sacred territory of the fierce Lakotas. To the geyser country with the longtime ally of the Arapahos, the Cheyenne.

But the four had never been this far out on the prairie.

It was the Thunder Moon, and the prairie teemed with life. Elk hid in the thick timber that fringed the streams. Deer could be flushed from the cottonwoods. Raccoons, possum, fox, coyotes, all called the prairie home. So did the wolf and the bear and the tawny cats with their sharp claws and fangs. Prairie dogs popped out of their burrows to whistle in alarm. Hawks soared on high, perpetually on the hunt. Birds sang and warbled and chirped. Vultures circled, doing their aerial dance of the dead.

It was the Thunder Moon, and their world was bountiful. Although they were far from Arapaho country, they were far from the country of tribes who might do them harm.

They felt safe traveling farther.

Two mornings later they were wending through a maze of rolling hillocks and gullies. The scent of the green grass was strong in their nostrils, the warm breeze strong on their backs. Puffy white clouds floated in the blue sky.

The four friends came around a bend and beheld a ribbon of water. They drew rein to let their mounts drink.

Short Bull was in the lead, as was his habit, and he

was the first to swing down. He stretched, then froze, his brown eyes fixed on the soft earth at the water's edge. From his lips came two words that stiffened the others. "White men."

The evidence was plain. Tracks of shod horses pockmarked the ground. Only white men rode shod horses. Mixed with the hoofprints were footprints of men in hard-soled boots. Only white men wore boots.

Wolf's Tooth was the best tracker. He squatted and read the sign. "I count nine. They came from the southeast and went that way." He pointed to the north. Rising, he examined a circle of trampled grass. "This is where they camped for the night. See? That is where a heavy one slept. They broke camp at sunrise. They cannot be far."

"They camped here?" Plenty Elk said skeptically. "Then why was there no fire? White men always make fires."

"I only say what their sign tells me."

Right Hand was studying a large footprint in the mud. "This one is twice as deep as the others." He put his foot next to the track to demonstrate. "He must be as heavy as my horse."

"What are they doing here?" Short Bull wondered. "They are far from the trails whites use."

"Maybe they hunt buffalo," Wolf's Tooth said.

Plenty Elk snorted. "Only white men would come to hunt buffalo when most of the herds are to the south."

"White men are strange," Short Bull said.

"White men are dangerous," Wolf's Tooth added.

No one disagreed. They had never fought white men, but they had listened to warriors who did. White men were hairy and smelly and had bad manners. White men were clumsy and noisy and made their fires much too big. They also had guns that could shoot far. Most important of all, in close combat white men were surprisingly formidable.

Only a few whites had come west of the Muddy River, but more trickled across the prairie each summer, many bound for a distant land by the great salt sea. Some stayed. A few lived on the prairie. A few more lived deep in the mountains. Some adopted Indian ways.

These nine came from the east, from where their kind reportedly lived in stone lodges and went about in carts such as the whites used to bring supplies to the rendezvous in the days of the beaver hunters.

All this the four friends knew, and more.

"I say we count coup on them," Short Bull proposed.

The others looked at him.

"Wolf's Tooth says there are nine," Plenty Elk reminded him.

"So?"

"They will have guns," Right Hand said.

"So?"

"So it does no good to count coup if you are killed counting it. We want to live to see our lodges again."

Short Bull made a noise of mild disgust. "Are we stupid that we let them see us and shoot us? No. We stalk them. We wait. When one or two separate from the rest, we strike. We count coup. We take their horses and their weapons. We return to our people and they sing of our courage. You get to wear feathers in your hair as I do."

"It appeals to me," Wolf's Tooth said.

Plenty Elk didn't hide his dislike of the idea. "There are things you do not do if you have sense.

You do not kick a skunk. You do not poke a sleeping bear with a stick. You do not hunt nine white men with guns."

"I will only do it if the rest of you do," Right Hand said.

Short Bull stepped to his horse. "Mount and we will follow them. They cannot be far ahead."

"Wait," Plenty Elk said. "Did you hear my words?"

"I heard the words of an old woman in the skin of a young man. Do you want to be a warrior, or would you rather cook and sew?"

"I want to go on breathing."

"Who of us does not? You make of these whites more than they are. They will fall to our arrows and knives as would an Ute or a Nez Perce."

"Stay here if you want," Wolf's Tooth said. "We will come get you when we have counted coup."

With a sharp gesture of annoyance, Plenty Elk stepped to his animal. "Where you three go, I go. That is how it has always been. That is how it will always be."

"Then stop complaining." Short Bull reined up the gully. He rode with his lance at his side. His grip showed he was ready to throw it at an instant's need.

The white men had followed the twists and turns of the gully for a long way. Finally their trail led up out of it—only to enter a dry wash and follow its serpentine windings.

"They do not want to be seen, these whites," Wolf's Tooth said.

"They hide from war parties," Right Hand noted.

The four young Arapahos went around a bend. Ahead was an oval hollow roughly an arrow's flight from side to side. They could see that the tracks crossed and went up and over the far slope. They kneed their horses and were halfway across when Short Bull's pinto pricked its ears and whinnied.

As if that were a signal, figures materialized on the hollow's rim. Nine men, all bristling with weapons, half wearing buckskins and most with beards. Sunlight glinted off rifle barrels and illuminated tobacco-stained teeth bared in vicious grins.

The four young warriors drew rein, startled.

"They were waiting for us," Plenty Elk said. "They knew we were following them and lured us into a trap."

One of the white men came down into the bowl. He wore a wide-brimmed black hat. He sauntered toward them with a casual, insolent air, his rifle in the crook of an elbow. He was no taller than the Arapahos but he was twice as broad, with shoulders wider than any man they had ever seen. His beard and hair were the color of a mountain lion's hide, and his eyes were as flint. He stopped, spat a dark juice on the ground, and said a few strange words.

"We do not speak your tongue, white man," Short Bull said.

The man cocked his head, his grin widening. "You Dog Eaters, yes?"

Their shock was considerable.

Right Hand recovered first and answered. "Yes. We are Arapaho. You speak our language?"

"I talk your tongue little," the white man said. "It many winters since last talk."

"How can a white man know our tongue?"

"Before you born, boy, I trap beaver. I find Arapaho warrior caught in ice. I help him."

"Why are you in Arapaho country?" Short Bull demanded.

"Your country?" The white man laughed. "This land no Arapaho. This land no Cheyenne. No Sioux. No Blackfeet. This land buffalo. This land prairie dogs."

"What do you do here?" Short Bull persisted.

A gleam came into the white man's flinty eyes. "We hunt."

"The big herds have gone south," Right Hand said. "Come back in three moons and the plain will be covered with them."

"We not hunt buffalo," the white man responded. "We hunt hair."

The four Arapahos looked at one another in mild confusion.

"Hair?" Plenty Elk said.

"Hair," the white man said again. He opened a pouch and reached inside. Very slowly, chuckling all the while, he drew his hand out and extended his arm so they could see what he was holding.

"Scalps!" Plenty Elk exclaimed.

The white man had a string of half a dozen on a length of rope. Most were long and all were black and none left any doubt as to the race of those who lost them.

"Indian scalps," Wolf's Tooth growled.

"This what we hunt. This how we live." The white man touched one. "This Otoe." He plucked at another. "This Pawnee." Yet another. "This Cheyenne woman."

Short Bull shifted toward his friends. He said one word, quietly. "Flee." Then he whipped around, raising his spear arm as he turned and tensed for the throw.

The boom of the white man's rifle was like thunder. At the blast, the lower half of Short Bull's face dissolved in a spray of skin and bone and blood, and he was catapulted off the back of his horse. He flew head over heels and came down with a thud.

The other three Arapahos scattered.

From the rim, the rest of the white men opened up. Some were laughing.

Right Hand bent low and streaked toward the west rim, but he barely brought his sorrel to a gallop when there was a *splat* and one of its eyes was no longer there. He clutched at the mane as the horse went into a roll. At the last moment he tried to throw himself clear and something struck his head a powerful blow that sent him plunging into a black pit.

Wolf's Tooth and Plenty Elk wheeled their animals and raced back the way they came. Hornets buzzed their ears. Suddenly Wolf's Tooth's shoulder burst in a shower of blood. He swayed and would have fallen if not for Plenty Elk, who reined in close and leaned over to steady him. Then they were in the gully and flew like the wind.

Behind them, the white man with the flinty eyes howled with fury.

Chapter Two

Green was the color of life. Green was the color of the Manitoa in all things. Green was the color most revered by the Nansusequa. Once, they were a proud and peaceful people, living deep in the virgin woodland of the East. Now there were only five Nansusequa left. The rest had been massacred by outraged whites. It didn't matter that the whites were to blame for the outrage; they wanted the land the Nansusequa lived on for themselves.

One family escaped the slaughter. Their peace chief, Wakumassee, fled with his wife and son and daughters. Their flight took them to the Mississippi River and across a nigh-endless sea of grass. After much hardship, they wound up at the base of emerald foothills, bumps compared to the snowbound peaks beyond that reared majestically miles high into the sky.

Fate brought them to a remote valley where Nate King befriended them and invited them to stay. Grateful beyond measure, they accepted. Every day Wakumassee gave thanks for the gift of King's friendship and for the happiness of having a place where his loved ones were safe. A haven far removed from the greed and bigotry that cost the Nansusequa so dearly.

It was a sobering thought; Waku and his family were the last of their kind, the last of the People of the Forest. For untold winters his people had lived in harmony with the green world around them and thrived. Then along came the white man. To their kind, the land wasn't a friend to be nurtured and cherished; it was property to be owned and used as the whites saw fit. When Waku first met them, it had taken a while for him to understand their way of seeing the world. When he finally did, he had been shocked to his core.

To be fair, not all whites were that way. Nate King wasn't. Shakespeare McNair wasn't. There were others, whites who regarded the world much as the Nansusequa did, as a precious gift to be treated with the utmost respect.

Now, drawing rein on the horse Nate King had given him, Waku gazed out over the vast rolling prairie and breathed deep of the grass-scented air. The warm sun on his face, the wind that stirred his long black hair—life was good again.

"Why have we stopped, husband?" asked Tihik-anima. Her green dress, like his green buckskins, were symbols of their devotion to Manitoa. "Have you seen something I haven't? Is there danger?"

Waku grunted. His wife tended to worry. But then, it was his opinion, based on many winters of marriage, that if women didn't have something to fret about, they made something up so they could. An opinion he kept to himself. "Be at peace, woman. All is well."

"Is it?" asked Tenikawaku, their oldest daughter, who had seen but seventeen winters. She bobbed her head at two of their party who had fallen behind.

Mikikawaku, at twelve the youngest, giggled. "Our brother spends more time with her than he does with us."

The brother she referred to was Degamawaku. At nineteen winters, he was as lithe and tawny as a cougar. He had the dark hair and dark eyes of the Nansusequa, and at the moment those eyes were on the white girl who rode beside him.

Evelyn King was close to Tenikawaku's age. She wore buckskins and moccasins and had a Hawken rifle cradled in her left arm and a pair of pistols tucked under a leather belt. Vitality gleamed in her green eyes, the same vitality that made her every movement as fluid as the graceful leaps of an antelope. "Look at me, Dega."

Degamawaku was puzzled. Why did she tell him to look at her when he already was? He was trying hard to master the white tongue, but it was proving as easy as wrestling a mud-slick snake. "I look."

"Here I am, wearing buckskins instead of a dress and traipsing around the prairie with you and your family. You'd never think to look at me that two years ago I had it fixed in my head that I was going to move back to the States."

"The States?"

"Yes. Remember? That's what my people call the land east of what you call the Father of Rivers. I was bound and determined to be a city girl and spend the rest of my days in civilized society."

Dega wasn't sure what all of that meant. He seemed to recall that whites called their villages "cities." What appalled him was the idea that she wanted to leave the mountains. "You still want go?"

Evelyn shook her head. "No. I've changed my mind. I've decided to stay out here."

"Why?"

Evelyn glanced away. She wasn't about to tell him of the strange feelings that had come over her lately, feelings the likes of which she never felt, feelings she *only* felt when she was around him or thinking about him.

"Why?" Dega asked again to show her he was genuinely interested.

Evelyn shrugged. "It's just one of those things. We think we know what we want when we don't. I reckon if we all knew our own minds as well as we like to think we do, we wouldn't make as many mistakes."

Dega tried to link her words into some semblance of meaning. As best he could work it out, she was saying that it was important to think. "True," he agreed. Given his limited grasp of her tongue, he had found that simple answers were best.

Evelyn smiled. "Have you noticed how much alike we are? Oh, I know you're red and I'm white, and you're a guy and I'm a girl. But deep down we have a lot in common."

Dega uttered the first thing that popped into his head. "We both have noses and feet."

Peals of mirth rippled from Evelyn. "Goodness gracious, the things you come up with. You're a hoot, Dega, and that's no lie."

Dega remembered being told once that a "hoot" was the sound an owl made. But since he hadn't made an owl sound he must be missing her meaning. "I hoot?"

"It means you make me smile."

"That good, yes?" Dega asked. His people had long believed that making others happy was one of the reasons they came into the world. Making Evelyn happy was especially important to him.

"That's very good." Evelyn glanced away again. She was becoming much too brazen, she told herself. Never once, by word or deed, had Dega so much as hinted that he cared for her any more deeply than he cared for his sisters.

"I be glad you come hunt," Dega remarked.

"That's another thing. I've never been much of a hunter. Oh, I've killed for the supper pot. But I never went on a buffalo hunt with the Shoshones even though my mother and uncle practically begged me."

"My father want buffalo meat." Dega had been perfectly content to stay in King Valley and spend every spare moment he could with Evelyn. Then his father took it into his head to go hunt buffalo.

"Blame Shakespeare McNair. He went on and on about how exciting it is to bring down a big buff, and he got your pa all excited." Evelyn gestured. "Now here we are."

So long as she was there, Dega didn't care where they were. "Here," he said happily.

"It makes you wonder, doesn't it?"

"What?"

"How life works out sometimes. We're walking along minding our own business and life kicks us in the britches."

Confusion racked Dega. He remembered that "britches" was a white word for "pants," and that "life" referred to being alive, but he couldn't fathom what being alive had to do with being kicked in the pants. So he did what he often did when she confused him; he smiled and repeated what she had just said. "In the britches."

Evelyn loved his smile. She had never told him

that, but he had the nicest teeth. Strange that she should notice. To her best recollection, she'd never paid much attention to teeth before. "My pa likes to say it's the Almighty's way of keeping us humble."

"Humble?"

"You know. Meek and mild and respectful."

"Respectful?"

"Yes. When you treat another person the way you'd want them to treat you. Nice. Friendly. With respect."

Dega brightened. At last something he understood. "Respect be good. Nansusequa believe respect all things."

"A fine philosophy as far as it goes. But how do you respect a bear about to eat you? Or a hostile about to slit your throat?" Evelyn could think of a host of other instances.

Dega was amazed at how her mind worked. It was always bouncing around all over the place. "Can respect bear. Just not let bear eat you."

Evelyn chuckled. "True enough, I suppose. But the last thing on my mind when something is trying to fill its belly with mouthfuls of me is treating it with respect. I'd rather shoot it." She caught herself, and shook her head. "Listen to me. I sound more like my brother every day, don't I?"

Dega answered as honestly as he knew how. "Brother sound like man. You sound like woman."

"I certainly hope so, you charmer you."

For the life of him, Dega couldn't recall what a charmer was. She was smiling, though, so he figured it must be a good thing. "Me great charmer."

More mirth spilled from Evelyn. She liked his sense of humor almost as much as she liked his teeth. "You know, I've never met anyone I can talk to as freely as I can talk to you."

"Talking you much nice," Dega said. Inside he cringed at his poor use of the white tongue. It was so hard to master. His father said it was because the Nansusequa tongue and the white tongue were so unlike. In the Nansusequa language, a word had one meaning and one meaning only. In the white language a word might have five meanings and each was shaded differently so that it must be used exactly right or it made no sense. Recently he had begun to despair of ever learning it well enough to make Evelyn proud.

"I wonder what it is about you," Evelyn said. Secretly, she had begun to suspect and the suspicion troubled her. She told herself she was too young. She told herself she had no interest in growing attached to someone. She told herself she was just being silly. Then she would look at him and something stirred deep down inside, something that never stirred before. She shook her head in annoyance.

"You all right?" Dega had found that her face often gave away her moods much better than her words did.

"I couldn't be happier." The devil of it was, Evelyn truly couldn't. She liked being with him more than she liked just about anything. Yet more reason for her to be troubled.

Evelyn took a few slow breaths to compose herself and saw that the rest of the family had stopped. She brought her mare to a halt and wondered why Teni and Miki were grinning.

Waku said, "We find buffalo soon, you think, Evelyn King?"

"There's no predicting," Evelyn replied. "At this time of year most are to the south, but there's always some that stick around. I'm surprised we haven't come across a few by now." She paused. "There's no need to be so formal. Just call me Evelyn. I get to call you Waku, don't I?" She liked the custom they had of allowing those who were near and dear to them to use a short version of their name. Their full names were a mouthful.

"I hope we find buffalo soon." The hunt had been Waku's idea. His wife had seen a buffalo robe that belonged to the wife of Zach King and mentioned that she would like to have a robe of her own one day. He'd taken that as a hint, and here they were.

A gust of wind against Evelyn's back prompted her to swivel in the saddle. To the west, dark clouds coiled and writhed like so many snakes. A thunderhead was moving in. It might pass north of them and it might not. She pointed and said, "We need to find shelter before that hits."

"You do not like rain?" Waku asked.

"I like it just fine. It's the storm I can do without. I've been caught in one or two prairie storms, and believe you me, it's like being caught in the end of the world. The rain falls in buckets, the wind is fit to blow you over, and then there's all that lightning."

Waku thought she exaggerated, but he used his heels and tugged on the lead rope to the packhorse.

Dega studied the dark clouds. They didn't appear particularly ominous, but he had learned to trust Evelyn's judgment. If she was worried, they should be worried. In his own tongue he said, "We would be wise to do as she advises, Father."

Motioning at the expanse of green that stretched to the eastern horizon, Waku said, "Show me where."

For as far as the eye could see there was flat, flat and more flat. Not so much as a single tree to the east, north or south.

Ahead, dirt mounds sprouted out of the earth.

A prairie dog town, Evelyn realized, and was about

to say they should give it a wide berth when Waku reined to the right to go around. She did the same. Out of the corner of her eye she admired Dega's handsome profile. He glanced at her, and she quickly averted her gaze and hoped she wasn't blushing.

Evelyn couldn't say exactly when, but a change had come over her. She was different somehow. She'd asked her mother about it, and her mother smiled knowingly and said she was on the cusp of womanhood, and that all women went through it. Which didn't make the changes any less disturbing.

A sound filled the air, a rattle like that of dry seeds in a gourd.

Alarm spiked through Evelyn. She had forgotten. Prairie dog towns were home to more than prairie dogs. They were also home to creatures that fed on the prairie dogs. Creatures like ferrets—and rattlesnakes. Even as she realized what the sound signified, her mare whinnied and reared. Evelyn grabbed at the saddle, but she was too slow. She was unhorsed.

The jolt of hitting the ground jarred Evelyn hard. She heard Dega and the others cry out, and she went to roll over so she could push to her feet.

The next instant a reptilian head reared, its mouth spread wide, its fangs bared.

Chapter Three

His last name was Venom. Those who knew him said the name fit his nature like a tight sock, but they never said it to his face.

Venom had a first name, which he never used. It was Nadine. If anyone else used it he kicked their teeth in. He hated it. He hated a lot of things. He hated preachers because they had their heads in the clouds. He hated kids because they were sniveling brats. He hated women because they put on airs. He hated dogs because they were always sniffing the hind ends of others dogs, and he hated cats because they were always rubbing against him and he couldn't abide being touched by anything or anyone unless it was a woman he paid for.

Venom hated Mexicans. He hated blacks except when it suited his purpose. He hated Indians, all Indians, with a fierce hate born of the loss of his father to a barbed shaft when he was seven. He hated Indians so much that when he drifted down to Santa Fe after the beaver trade petered out and met a man by the name of Kirker who offered him a job scalping redskins for money, he eagerly accepted.

The Mexican government was paying bounty for

Apache scalps. Good money. A hundred dollars for a warrior's hair, fifty dollars for the hair of a female, twenty-five for the hair of what Venom liked to call "Apache gnats."

Kirker had formed a company of scalpers made up of men who could hold their own against the most formidable warriors on the continent. Men without scruples. Men who regarded killing Indians as exterminating vermin. Men who could take a squalling Apache infant and bash its brains out on the rocks.

Venom fit right in. He took to his new profession with a zeal that at first amused and then troubled the hard men he worked with. One day he went out and slaughtered a harmless Pima family—father, mother and three small children—and turned their scalps in for the bounty, claiming their hair belonged to Chiricahua Apaches.

That angered Kirker. Not because Venom had done it; Kirker did it, too. Kirker was angry because Venom bragged about it. The Mexican government turned a blind eye to the slaughter of innocent Indians so long as it was done quietly. Kirker didn't want Venom spoiling a good thing. He told Venom to scalp-hunt by the rules.

Venom said the rules be damned, he would kill any redskin he pleased. When Kirker told him that if he couldn't follow orders he couldn't be in Kirker's company, Venom formed his own company. Within a year his company was earning more bounty than Kirker's, but the more scalps they took, the harder it became. The merest whisper that Venom and his men were coming, and every Indian for a hundred miles, hostile and peaceful, melted away until it was safe to come out again.

It got so that killing Indians didn't bring in enough

money. Venom started killing long-haired Mexicans and claiming their scalps belonged to Indians.

Then Venom heard that the government of Texas was offering bounty money for Comanche scalps. He figured that Comanches would be easier to catch and kill than Apaches, so off to Texas he and his company went. He figured wrong. Soon they were back to their old tricks of killing friendly Indians and Mexicans and even a few whites with long black hair.

One evening Venom and his company came on a lone Mexican rider, a youth in a fine sombrero and expensive clothes, riding a grand bay. An entire silver mine went to decorate the youth's saddle. The youth's dark hair, unfortunately for the youth, fell well past his shoulders.

Venom pretended to be friendly. The boy claimed to be related to the alcade of San Antonio, but Venom didn't believe him. In his eyes all Mexicans were born liars.

So Venom pointed into the distance and asked if that was a buffalo he saw, and when the youth turned to see for himself, Venom buried his knife between the boy's shoulder blades. He helped himself to the scalp—and the grand bay and the fancy silver saddle, besides.

All went well for a couple of weeks. Then Venom heard that the law was after him. The boy had been telling the truth about the alcade, and someone got word to the authorities.

Texas was suddenly too hot for Venom. He decided to hell with Texans and took his company east to St. Louis for a much-deserved debauch. Whiskey, women and cards soon ate up the last peso in their pokes.

Venom's company headed west again after more scalps. Since Venom couldn't return to Texas, he headed for the province of New Mexico. He had barely started out when inspiration struck.

Friendly Pawnees rode up to Venom's camp and asked if he had any liquor they could buy or trade for. Venom smiled and invited them to sit by his fire. He passed around a flask and while the Pawnees were sipping and smiling, his men pounced.

Just like that Venom had seven new scalps. It occurred to him that if he sought Indians out on the way to Santa Fe, preferably the peaceful ones who rarely fought back, he'd have a lot of scalps to turn in. In fact, if he did it right, his packs would practically bulge with bounty.

So far he had twenty-three scalps.

Venom wasn't happy. He paced back and forth, his jaw muscles twitching, and glowered at his company. "You call yourselves scalp hunters? What gall. We had four bucks in our sights and you let two of them get away."

A heavyset man named Potter nervously shifted his weight from one pudgy leg to the other. "They were too quick for us, boss."

"Speak for yourself, you tub of lard," Venom snapped. "And since when is a man on a horse faster than a bullet?"

"We hit one," declared a tall bundle of whipcord and bone. "That should count for something."

"Not when they don't go down, Tibbet." Venom gestured in contempt. "Here I thought I'd hired the cream of the Injun killers, and all of you are plumb worthless."

Of the eight men, five withered under his glare. Three didn't.

One was called Logan, and he had been hinting of late that he would make a better leader than Venom.

The other two were as alike as peas in a pod, with good reason; they were twins. Both had straw-colored hair and blue eyes and freckled complexions. The Kyler brothers hailed from Kentucky. That was all anyone knew about them. That, and they would kill anyone or anything, anytime, anywhere. Now one of the twins said in his slow Southern drawl, "My brother and me don't much like bein' insulted, Mr. Venom."

His sibling bobbed his chin. "That's right. We did our part, and there ain't a coon here who can claim different."

"Did I blame you? Either of you?" Venom retorted. "You're the best shots in the outfit. If you had shot at the two who got away, they wouldn't have got away. You never miss."

"Oh, now and then we do," said one of the twins.

"Remember that Comanch that time?" said the other.

Venom snorted. "He was five hundred yards away. You'd need a damn cannon to hit something that far off."

"We've done it before," said the first twin.

"These rifles of ours ain't for show nor ballast," said the other. "But the sun was in our eyes that day."

"You don't need to convince me." Venom never antagonized the pair if he could help it. Secretly he thought they were as dumb as tree stumps, but they were also quite deadly.

"Do we go after those two?" asked Rubicon. He was black. Venom tolerated him because Rubicon was the best tracker Venom ever came across.

"Do buffalo roll in their own piss? Of *course* we go after them. But there's no hurry." Venom stepped to where the two dead ones had been laid out. Drawing his skinning knife, he tested the edge on his thumb and smiled when a thin red line appeared.

No one objected. They knew he liked to do the cutting. Even those he didn't kill he often scalped himself. Not that he kept the scalps if he didn't make the kill. He just liked to lift hair. That, and one other thing he liked.

Squatting next to the Arapaho who had done most of the talking, Venom inserted the tip a quarter inch from the hairline and carefully cut a straight line from brow to brow. "Smell that? This buck used bear fat to slick his hair."

"A lot of Injuns do," Tibbet said.

"Smelliest critters on God's green earth," declared Logan. He spat a wad of tobacco and picked at his armpit. "If it ain't buffalo fat, it's horse piss. How their women can stand to be near them is a wonder."

"I had me a squaw once," Potter said. "An Otoe, she was. Scrawny little thing, but she kept herself clean. Well, except for the lice. But I don't mind lice much. I've got some myself."

Venom wasn't paying much attention to their prattle. He was engrossed in the scalping. He always did it a certain way. He started at the front and worked clear around, prying and peeling until he could lift the entire scalp just as easy as could be. Some scalp hunters did it in a rush and didn't bother to take all the hair. Not him. He always took all of it.

There was something else that Venom did. Something none of the others would do, ever. They were used to him doing it, but it still gave some of them queasy stomachs to watch, and they were men who did not get queasy easy.

Venom cut around an ear and felt the edge of the knife scrape on the skull bone. That only happened when he pressed too hard. He eased up slightly, enough that the blade seemed to glide from the ear to the base of the neck and then around to the other side. As he cut, he licked his lips in anticipation.

Potter did more fidgeting. "Can I ask you something, boss?"

"So long as it won't make me mad." Venom didn't like being distracted while he cut.

"Why do you do it?"

"What? Lift scalps? I told you about my pa, didn't I? How those damn Creeks did him in? Ever since, I've made it my life's work to kill as many redskins as I can before I get planted."

"No, not that." Potter shifted again. "The other thing. Why do you do the other thing?"

Venom cut around the other ear. He didn't pull on the hair, as some did, not yet, anyway. Experience had taught him that he wasted a lot of blood that way.

"I mean, it's none of my business, I know," Potter babbled on. "But me and some of the others have wanted to ask for a long time. You've never said, exactly."

"You should try it," Venom said. "Then you'd understand."

Potter put a hand to his ample middle. "No sir. Not me. I don't draw the line at much, but that there is one line I refuse to cross."

"You drink water, don't you?"

"Only when there's nothing stronger."

"Milk, then? You drink milk?"

Potter shrugged. "Now and then. I liked it more when I was a boy. My ma put it on my oatmeal and she'd slice up peaches and—"

"Do I care what your damn mother did?" Venom interrupted. "We were talking about drinking. You're partial to rye, as I recollect."

"What's your point?"

Glancing up, Venom wagged his knife, causing scarlet drops to spatter his boot. "My point, jackass, is that you drink what you like and I drink what I like. There's your answer."

"But it's not drinking you do. It's more like—" Potter scrunched up his face. "It's more like sucking."

"Drink or suck, it's all the same."

"Begging your pardon, boss, but a drink is when it's in a bottle or a glass. Not when it's skin."

Logan said, "I'd as soon suck swamp water as what you do. How'd you ever get started, anyhow?"

"It was back when I was hunting Apaches, before I formed my own company," Venom explained. "Kirker and me and some others were in the desert, tracking Chiricahuas. Little did we guess at the time but the red bastards led us out there on purpose, thinking we'd die of thirst. And we damn near did. We ran out of water and separated to hunt for a tank or a spring, anything." He chuckled at the memory. "Do you know what saved me?"

No one hazarded a guess.

"I'll tell you. It was a Chiricahua buck. He'd hid behind a cactus and didn't think I'd spotted him, but he made the mistake of blinking. I scalped him and it started to bleed, and the blood set me to thinking how thirsty I was, and the next thing I knew, I stuck a finger in my mouth and sucked the blood off."

"Injun blood," said Calvert. He was typically the quietest of the bunch.

"Wet is wet," Venom retorted. "Just the little I sucked made me feel better so I smeared more on my finger and sucked that off." He bent over the Arapaho and peeled off the scalp as he might peel an orange. Then, holding it up for them to see, he smacked his lips. "I reckon you know what I did next."

Potter turned away. "I can't watch. It makes me sick to my stomach every single time."

"You damned weak sister." Venom held the scalp in both hands so the blood-soaked skin side faced him. Then, slowly, methodically, he commenced to suck on the skin and to swallow with relish.

"You couldn't pay me to do that," Tibbet remarked.

"I'd die of thirst first," the man they called Ryson said.

Venom stopped sucking and grinned, his mouth and chin smeared bright scarlet. "Potter's not the only weak sister. But that's all right. It leaves more of the sauce for me."

"The sauce?" Tibbet repeated.

"The blood, stupid." Venom sucked, and beamed, his teeth gleaming bright red. "It's too bad they don't sell blood in bottles. I'd drink that before I'd drink whiskey."

"Don't take this the wrong way, boss," Potter said, "but you're loco."

Nadine Venom laughed.

Chapter Four

Evelyn King froze every muscle in her body. One bite from the rattler and its deadly poison would course through her veins. Even if her friends sucked out the poison there was no guarantee she would live. She stared into the vertical slits of the angry serpent's eyes, and a chill ran down her spine. It was poised to sink its fangs into her flesh.

There was the twang of a bowstring. An arrow cored the rattler's head and imbedded itself in the ground, pinning the rattlesnake to the earth, and the snake, although dead, went into a paroxysm of thrashing and coiling and rattling its tail.

Evelyn swallowed and let out the breath she had been holding. Strong hands gripped her and pulled her to her feet. Her eyes met those of the archer and what she saw in them sent a different kind of tingle down her spine.

Dega thought his heart would burst when the snake went to strike. He had notched a shaft and let fly almost before his brain realized what his body was doing. Half fearful Evelyn had already been bitten, he vaulted from his horse and helped her up. "You be all right?" he anxiously asked.

"A little bruised, is all." Evelyn's arms were warm

where he touched them. "Thank you for saving me. You're awful quick with that bow."

"I worry—" Dega said, and stopped. His voice sounded husky and his throat was oddly tight. Letting go, he stepped back and slung his bow over his shoulder. "I glad you no hurt."

The others brought their mounts in close. Waku leaned down and put a hand on Evelyn's shoulder.

"Are you sure you are not hurt, Evelyn King?"

"I'm fine. Really."

Teni had caught the mare before it could run off, and now she held out the reins. "Here you are," she said in the Nansusequa tongue.

"Thank you." Evelyn felt slightly embarrassed. The mishap wasn't her fault, but being unhorsed was always unsettling. She checked that her Hawken hadn't been damaged in the fall, then climbed back on.

Dega placed his foot on the snake just below the head and extracted his arrow. It took some doing. The barbed tip became caught in the skull and he used his knife to pry it free. Wiping the shaft clean on the grass, he slid the arrow into his quiver.

Moving on, they stayed well shy of the prairie dog town. Twice they spotted rattlers sunning themselves.

It occurred to Evelyn that they should have brought the dead snake with them and chopped it up for supper. Not that she was all that partial to snake meat. She'd eaten it on occasion, but she much preferred venison or rabbit or squirrel. It wasn't that snake meat had a bad taste. In fact, it was quite good. It was the notion of eating *snake*. Crawly things were her least favorite creatures in all creation.

Toward the middle of the afternoon Dega brought his mount up next to the mare and rode at Evelyn's side until he mustered the courage to ask, "You like me, Ev-el-lyn?"

"I like you just fine," Evelyn admitted. "You're just about the best friend I've ever had."

"Friend." Dega had hoped she might like him a little bit more. He didn't have the white words to express what he wanted to say, and he was worried he might offend her if he didn't do it right.

"Someone you care for a great deal. Someone who means the world to you."

"I know what friend be."

Evelyn wondered why he sounded upset. "Why did you ask? Did you think I don't like you?"

"Oh. No. I know you like," Dega assured her. She had misunderstood. Added proof that he must be careful what he said and particularly how he said it. "I like you much, too."

"Did you have friends like me back in your village?" Evelyn asked without thinking, and regretted it when his face mirrored sadness.

"Many friends, yes."

Evelyn knew she should let it drop, but she wanted to know. "Female friends?"

Dega was thinking of the massacre, of the many relatives and friends he lost. "Many females, yes."

"Oh." Evelyn didn't like the sound of that. She wondered if maybe there had been a special girl, but she was afraid to ask.

Up ahead, Tihikanima looked back at them and then turned to her husband. "Will you like her as a daughter-in-law?"

In the distance were specks that might be large animals, and Waku was intent on learning if they were buffalo. "What are you talking about?"

"Dega and Evelyn. When they are husband and wife, she will be part of our family."

Waku tore his gaze from the specks to thoughtfully regard his wife. "Do you truly believe it will come to that?"

"Do you have eyes? She has touched our son's heart. You have only to look at his face when he looks at her."

Adopting a casual air, Waku gazed about them, making it a point to gaze behind them, as well. "I see no difference than when he looks at you or me."

Tihi indulged in an exaggerated sigh. "That is because you are a man. You are not sensitive to feelings, as women are."

"I am as sensitive as you." Waku was mildly offended. He took great pains to be the best husband and father he could be.

"Do you want her as your son's wife?"

"Why do you ask such a thing? Now, of all times?"

"The others will not hear us if we talk quietly."

"That is not what I meant." Waku would rather talk about it in the privacy of their lodge than out here on the prairie when he was trying to find buffalo.

"It will not be long, I tell you, before he decides to court her. Given how she feels about him, we have important decisions to make."

Resigned to the inevitable, Waku asked, "How do you know how she feels? Has she told you?"

"She does not need to. Do you think she came with us because she likes to butcher buffalo? No, she came to be with Dega. Have you not noticed that she spends every moment in his company? She cares for him, Waku. He cares for her. Are you ready to lose him?"

"If they marry, we do not lose a son. We gain a daughter," Waku said.

"Must I explain everything?" Tihi let out another

sigh. "What is the Nansusequa custom when a young man and a young woman bind hearts?"

"The woman comes to live in the lodge of the man and his parents," Waku answered.

"What is the white custom?"

"Eh?"

"Blue Water Woman is a Flathead, is she not? She took Shakespeare McNair as her man and lives in his lodge."

"Yes. So?"

"Winona is a Shoshone. She took Nate King for a husband. Do they live in a lodge with her people or do they live in Nate's lodge far from the Shoshones?"

"They live in his lodge, but—"

"Zachary King has married a white woman, Louisa. Do they live in the same lodge as Nate and Winona or do they have a lodge of their own?"

"They have their own lodge." Waku saw what she was getting at, and it troubled him.

"What makes you think Evelyn will be different? What makes you think she will come live with us? I suspect she will want to do as her parents and her brother and live in a lodge of her own."

Waku had looked forward to one day having his grown children and their families share his lodge. That had been the Nansusequa way since there were Nansusequa. It was why they built their lodges so large. Two or three or sometimes four generations all lived in the same dwelling, all devoted to one another, the old imparting their wisdom to the young, the young looking after the old when the old could no longer look after themselves.

Tihi had gone on. "I have something else for you to think about. We are the last of our kind. None of the other tribes live as we did. When our daughters grow of age and take husbands, they will probably go live with their men. We will be alone with no one to look after us."

Deep sorrow came over Waku. It was bad enough to be the last of the Nansusequa. To think that when he and his wife died, the Nansusequa way of life died with them—forever—was a sadness that surpassed all others.

"We cannot blame our children," Tihi said.

"We can't?"

"What else are they to do? With all our people slain they must look for mates elsewhere."

Waku's mood turned bitter. Usually he tried not to think of the fate of their people; it depressed him too much. So long as he focused on his family and what he could do to make their lives happier, he kept the sadness at bay.

Shaking himself, Waku straightened. Time enough later to ponder the future, he told himself. At the moment he was after buffalo. The stick figures had disappeared while he was talking to Tihi. He continued in that direction, hoping that whatever they were they hadn't gone far.

The vastness of the prairie staggered him.

All his life, Waku lived in the deep woods. The forest nurtured him. Its bounty enabled his people to thrive. It was everything; sanctuary, provider, mother. He'd never imagined a world with no forest, never conceived there was a sea of grass to rival the sea of trees.

Waku liked the mountains more than the plain. The mountains had their meadows and glades and clearings, but in many respects the high timber reminded him of the woods he had forsaken when he and his family fled.

"Waku?" Tihi said.

"I do not care to hear any more about Dega and Evelyn."

Tihi pointed. "What are those?"

Squinting against the glare of the afternoon sun, Waku spied more stick figures. These were to the north and moving south. They were moving fast and if they kept on would pass within a few arrow flights in front of them.

"Men on horses."

Waku had come to the same conclusion. Two riders, racing across the prairie as if their lives depended on it. He drew rein. "Everyone look there!" he shouted, in both Nansusequa and English.

Evelyn was debating the best way to ask Dega if there had ever been a girl he was particularly fond of. Twisting, she rose in the stirrups. "Warriors! I can't tell the tribe yet."

"They in hurry," Dega said.

Too much of a hurry, Evelyn thought. The pair were riding like the wind—or as if they were being pursued. She didn't see anyone else. "We should talk to them."

"Is that wise?" Waku asked. "Maybe they are our enemies."

"If there's a war party hereabouts, we need to find out." Evelyn checked that her Hawken and her pistols were loaded.

"One man is bent over," Waku mentioned.

Evelyn had noticed that, too. It looked as though he was hurt. The other warrior stayed at his side and reached out to him from time to time.

The pair changed direction, reining to the southeast, away from Waku and his family.

"They have seen us."

"Come on," Evelyn urged. The mare had been

held to a walk for so long that she was eager to let herself go.

"Wait!" Waku cried. He was worried that if anything happened to her, Nate King would blame him. Slapping his legs against his mount, he hastened after her. He had little chance of catching up. She had been riding since she was old enough to sit a horse; he'd only learned to ride recently.

"Evelyn!" Dega shouted, and gave chase. Her impulsive nature bothered him. She was constantly taking him by surprise.

Evelyn paid them no mind. She wasn't near enough to the two warriors to be in any danger. The wind whipping her hair, she urged the mare to go faster.

The warrior who appeared to be hurt caught sight of her and yelled to the other one.

Waving her rifle, Evelyn yelled at the top of her lungs, "Friend! I'm a friend!" She did the same in Shoshone and in Crow.

The pair were flying. If they understood her, they gave no indication.

Evelyn knew she should stop, but she kept going. Call it stubbornness. Call it curiosity. She wanted to talk to them, by sign language if no other way. She was aware of Dega thundering behind her and the rest of the family strung out after him.

The warrior who was bent over his horse seemed to be clinging on for dear life. The other warrior swiveled at the hips and raised both arms as if in supplication.

Puzzled, Evelyn waved. She realized the second warrior was holding something.

"Stop!" Dega frantically yelled.

Evelyn never had liked being told what to do.

"You must stop!"

A sharp retort was on the tip of Evelyn's tongue, but it died as it hit her exactly was the second warrior was doing. She glanced skyward and her skin crawled at the sight of a glittering shaft arcing out of the sky toward her.

"Evelyn!" Dega cried.

Evelyn had heartbeats in which to react. With a silent prayer she wrenched on the reins.

Chapter Five

Plenty Elk swiftly notched another arrow to his bow-string, but the young white woman drew rein when his arrow imbedded itself in the dirt near her horse. Those with her also stopped. He felt safe in lowering his bow and shoving the arrow back into his quiver.

He couldn't believe it when he first saw them. Indians all in green! And a white woman! This was a day of unexpected events. First the scalp hunters; now these others.

Plenty Elk did not know what the woman's intent was in giving chase. She might have been friendly, but she was well armed and he was not taking chances, not with his friend wounded. "Can you keep riding?"

"Yes." Wolf's Tooth gritted his teeth against the pain and tried not to think of all the blood he'd lost. He had been dizzy for a while, but the bout had passed. Now he was weak but not so weak that he couldn't ride. "Who were those people?"

"Strangers." Plenty Elk shouted to be heard above the pounding of hooves. "One of them was white."

"Maybe they are with the scalp men."

Plenty Elk doubted it. The scalp men would take

the hair of any Indians they came across, including those in green.

"Is there sign of them?"

Plenty Elk scoured the prairie to the north. "No." It puzzled him. He'd expected the scalp hunters to give determined chase.

The pair galloped on until their horses were lathered with sweat. A ribbon of cottonwoods along a narrow stream offered shade from the heat and water to clean Wolf's Tooth's wound. Plenty Elk cut a strip of buckskin from his friend's shirt to bandage it.

"There. Do not use the arm much and in a moon you will be almost healed. The bullet went all the way through. You were fortunate."

Wolf's Tooth placed his good hand on his hurt shoulder and grunted. "I do not feel fortunate."

Plenty Elk stepped to the stream. Kneeling, he washed his hands clean of the blood. "We must warn our people about the scalp men. We must warn our friends, the Cheyenne."

"We must kill them."

"When Tall Bull hears that his son is dead, he will raise a war party. He loved Short Bull very much."

"I want to go with them. I want to see the scalp men die with my own eyes," Wolf's Tooth declared.

"You cannot fight with one arm."

"I can use a knife. I can swing a tomahawk."

Plenty Elk wiped his hands dry on the grass. He went to his horse, opened a parfleche, and brought over a bundle wrapped in badger fur. Opening it, he held out a piece of pemmican. "Eat. You must keep your strength up. It is a long ride to our village."

"We should start back."

Plenty Elk selected another piece and bit off the end. Chewing, he said, "There is no hurry. There is no sign of the scalp men, and you need to build up your strength."

"I can ride."

Bobbing his head at their horses, Plenty Elk said, "They need rest, too." Both animals were hanging their heads in exhaustion.

Wolf's Tooth put his hand to his brow and closed his eyes. "I still can hardly believe it. Short Bull and Right Hand, gone. They were our best friends. We played together when we were small."

Plenty Elk couldn't believe it, either. It had happened so fast. "We were fools to track those men. I tried to talk Short Bull out of it. You heard me argue with him."

"He never listened to any words but his own."

"Right Hand did not want to do it, either. He only went along because the rest of us did."

"His woman will wail and cut herself."

"And her, heavy with child," Plenty Elk said glumly.

"She can go live with her parents. Or she can come to my lodge. I have always liked her."

"You would raise the child as your own?"

"Right Hand was my friend."

Plenty Elk stood. "I will take a look around." He walked through the cottonwoods to the edge of the grass. To the north, nothing. To the west, nothing. He checked the south, too, with the same result.

"Well?" Wolf's Tooth prompted upon his return.

"We are safe."

"You do not sound certain."

Plenty Elk squatted. He picked up a stick and poked at the dirt. "It was too easy."

"What was?"

"The scalp hunters should have come after us. They didn't. It worries me."

Wolf's Tooth leaned on his good arm and studied Plenty Elk. "You have always worried too much. When there is nothing to worry about, you worry about that."

"You do not worry enough."

"Did you see horses?"

"I told you. No one is after us."

"No. Not now. When the scalp men tried to kill us. Did you see their horses anywhere?"

"I saw only the scalp men."

"There is your answer. They had to run to their horses. We had too much of a start and they could not catch us."

Plenty Elk would like to think it was that simple. "It would be easy for them to track us."

Wolf's Tooth forgot himself, and shrugged. Wincing, he said, "Tracking takes time."

"It is daylight. Our tracks are fresh."

"You forget. They were white men. Few whites are good trackers."

"One of them had black skin," Plenty Elk reminded him. "And I have heard there are whites who can track as good as anyone."

"Worry they are tracking us if you want to." Wolf's Tooth eased onto his back and placed his arm over his eyes. "While you worry, I will rest. Wake me when the horses have recovered enough to head for our village."

Plenty Elk rose and went back to the edge of the prairie. Sitting with his back to a bole, he placed his bow across his legs. The sun was warm on his face, the wind stirred his hair. Somewhere in the cottonwoods a robin warbled. A yellow butterfly fluttered past.

The world was at peace, but the same could not be said of Plenty Elk's spirit. Again and again he searched the far horizon in all directions, and always it was the same. He would like to believe Wolf's Tooth was right. He would like to accept the fact they had escaped. But he had looked into the eyes of the scalp hunter who spoke their tongue, and what he saw had unnerved him. They were not normal eyes. Looking into them was like looking into the violent depths of a rabid animal.

Plenty Elk swallowed and licked his lips, and sighed. There was still no sign of anyone. Maybe Wolf's Tooth was right. He worried too much. Leaning back, he closed his eyes. He could use some rest, too. The deaths of his friends, the long ride, had drained him.

A cricket chirped. High in the sky a hawk screeched. A fly buzzed near his ear. The usual sounds of a usual day. Peaceful sounds. Plenty Elk drifted into a gray realm between wakefulness and sleep. Part of him wanted to doze off, but another part, the part that always worried, warned him he shouldn't. Despite what Wolf's Tooth said, it wasn't safe.

He fell asleep anyway.

Plenty Elk dreamed he was running. It was early morning, and fog blanketed the land. Something or someone was after him, but he couldn't see what or who it was. He kept looking over his shoulder, but all he saw were shadowy shapes—and glowing eyes. Eyes like wolves. He ran and he ran, but he couldn't outdistance them. They were always back there, always glowing bright with evil glee.

In his dream Plenty Elk tripped. Before he could rise, the shadowy shapes were on him. They bore him to the earth. Some pinned his arms while others pinned his legs. He struggled with all his might, but they were many and he was one. A knife appeared, sweeping out of the fog like a scythe. He tried to twist his head aside but a burning sensation filled his throat and he felt warm drops of blood trickle down his neck.

With a start, Plenty Elk sat up and gazed wildly about. He sucked air into his lungs and wiped the sweat from his brow with a sleeve.

"That was silly." Plenty Elk pushed to his feet. The prairie was still empty of life. He glanced at the sun and was surprised to note how high it had climbed. He had been asleep much too long.

The horses were dozing. Wolf's Tooth was still on his back, his arm over his eyes.

"Wake up. We must be on our way."

When Wolf's Tooth didn't stir, Plenty Elk walked over and went to nudge Wolf's Tooth's foot with his own. Only then did Plenty Elk see the ring of red around his friend's head. He took another step— and saw pink flesh where there should be hair.

Recoiling, Plenty Elk gripped the hilt of his knife. He had the blade halfway out when he was struck a terrible blow to the back of the head. Excruciating pain flooded through him. His senses swam, his legs grew weak, and his legs buckled. He came down hard on his knees. Struggling to stay conscious, he managed to draw his knife, only to have it kicked from his hand. Another blow, not quite as hard as the first, stretched him out on his side. Dimly, he was aware of being stripped of his weapons and having his legs tied at the knees and at the ankles. His hands, though, were left free. Why that should be mystified him until he was roughly rolled onto his back.

It was the black man. He had a rifle in one hand, a tomahawk in the other. A smile without warmth creased his cold features. Wedging the tomahawk under his belt, he leaned the rifle against a leg. Then his fingers flowed in fluid sign. 'When brain work, Dog Eater, we sign talk.'

Plenty Elk tried to swallow, but his mouth was dry. He looked at Wolf's Tooth, at the fate that soon awaited him, and felt great regret. He loved being alive. He did not want to die.

The black stared at him, waiting.

Plenty Elk wondered why he was still alive. Forcing his hands to move, he posed the question in sign.

'Big man want talk you.'

By "big man," Plenty Elk gathered that the black meant the man who spoke Arapaho. 'Question. Why he talk me?'

'He ask where you sit. He ask how many you people. He ask how many warriors. How many women. How many children.'

Fear filled Plenty Elk, not for himself but for his people. He resolved not to tell the scalp men where his village was or how many lived there, no matter what. 'I no sign talk.'

The black did a strange thing; he laughed. 'You talk. Him make all people talk.'

Plenty Elk didn't like the sound of that. The scalp men tortured as well as scalped. Truly, he told himself, they were evil.

Squatting, the black regarded him with amusement. 'Question. You called?'

Plenty Elk signed his name. 'Question. You?'

'No sign talk my name. I speak name.' The black touched his chest. "Rubicon," he said slowly.

"Ru-bi-con," Plenty Elk repeated. 'You first black man I see.'

'I last black man you see.'

Plenty Elk sank his cheek to the grass and closed his eyes. The pain had lessened a little and he could think again. Unless he did something, quickly, he wouldn't live to greet the next dawn. But other than try and grab Rubicon's rifle, what could he do? He looked up at his captor. 'Question. Why you take hair? Take hair bad.'

Rubicon held his right hand out from his chest and curled his thumb and index finger to make a near-complete circle.

It was the sign for money.

Hope flared in Plenty Elk's breast. 'Question. You cut rope I give you my horse? You sell horse. Have money.'

'Your hair more money.'

In the distance hooves drummed.

Plenty Elk stiffened. It must be the rest of the scalp hunters. He started to lower his hands to the rope around his legs. Without warning Rubicon sprang and swung the stock of his rifle in a tight arc. Plenty Elk nearly cried out. His ribs felt as if they had caved in.

"Don't get no ideas, redskin."

Plenty Elk understood the warning tone if not the words. He gazed through the trees to the west, seeking sign of his impending doom. They would torture him and kill him and lift his hair, and there wasn't a thing he could do. In his frustration and helplessness, he raised a loud lament to the sky.

Rubicon rose. Smirking, he cradled his rifle. "Listen to you howl. That's your death chant, ain't it?"

The drumming hooves slowed as they neared the cottonwoods. Plenty Elk girded himself and dived at Rubicon's legs, but the black man was too quick for him and leaped out of reach.

Snarling, Rubicon raised his rifle to hit Plenty Elk again.

That was when the brush crackled and out of the trees came the last person Plenty Elk expected: the young white woman.

Chapter Six

Evelyn King drew rein when the arrow thudded into the earth, and she watched the two warriors gallop off. She still didn't know which tribe they belonged to. They weren't Blackfeet or Sioux, or they would have tried harder to kill her or take her captive.

Degamawaku's heart had leaped into his throat when he saw the glittering shaft arc out of the sky. For a few harrowing moments he thought it would bury itself in Evelyn. His relief when it missed was so profound that he trembled from head to toe. Drawing rein, he forced his throat to work. "Be careful, please. You almost be killed."

"I don't think so," Evelyn said. "I don't think he was trying to kill me, just scare me."

"He scare me."

The others came trotting up, Wakumassee and Tihikanima and Tenikawaku and Mikikawaku.

"Why did you chase them?" Waku demanded. He liked the white girl, liked her a lot, but at times she did rash things.

"I wanted to talk to them," Evelyn explained. "I still do. Didn't you see that one of them was hurt?"

"They not want your help." Waku considered the arrow the warrior let fly a distinct hint.

"They were afraid of us."

"*They* afraid of *us*?" Waku repeated in some amazement.

Evelyn rose in the stirrups and surveyed the vast extent of plain to the north. "The important thing is who hurt that warrior? They must have run into enemies. If there's a war party somewhere close, we need to know."

Waku hadn't thought of that. "If there is war party near, we must go far away."

"What if they're between us and the mountains?" Evelyn shook her head. "They could be anywhere. We need to find out who and how many and where those two warriors last saw them." She gigged the mare.

Dega was aghast. She had just escaped being shot with an arrow and here she was going after the men who shot at her. He glanced at his father in mute appeal and saw that he was just as dumbfounded.

Tihi didn't like this one bit. "What is that foolish girl doing?"

"She thinks we need to talk to the two warriors," Waku said. "She says there could be enemies close by."

"Then we should return to the mountains. Out here on the prairie it is too open. We are too exposed."

"I agree with Mother," Tenikawaku said. She never wanted to come hunt buffalo in the first place. She was perfectly content to stay in King Valley where they were safe.

Little Minikawaku said nothing. She did not understand any of this, but she trusted her parents to do what was best.

"Stop her, Waku," Tihi said. "Call to her."

"She would not listen. She is headstrong, that one."

Tihi smothered a tart reply. At moments like these she wished her husband was a bit more forceful, even if it wasn't the Nansusequa way. The People of the Forest believed in living in harmony with everyone where possible. They exalted reason over confrontation, peace over violence. Unfortunately, as they had learned to their bitter sorrow, not everyone shared their ideals.

"We must go after her," Waku said. "Her father and mother have been exceptionally kind to us."

"She is a child in a woman's body," Tihi said in uncharacteristic anger. "I am grateful for what her parents have done for us, but they have not raised her right."

"They are not Nansusequa."

Dega was impatient to catch up to Evelyn. A dutiful son would wait for his father and mother to finish their talk, but he slapped his horse's legs and hurried off.

"Let us go," Waku said, and followed him.

Reluctantly Tihi goaded her animal on. She was not in the best of spirits. The long ride to the prairie had given her a lot of time to think, and her thoughts ran in troubling channels. As grateful as she was to Nate and Winona King—and she *was* sincerely grateful—she was not so sure she liked the idea of her son taking their daughter for his wife. There was the issue of Dega leaving their lodge. She was certain Evelyn would insist on it. And their children; would they be raised in the Nansusequa way or the white way? No, the more Tihi considered it, the more convinced she became that her son should not marry Evelyn King.

A jab of her heels quickened her mount's gait so that she passed her husband and her daughters and caught up to her eldest child. Dega was staring intently after Evelyn, so love-struck it would amuse her were the consequences not so serious.

"You would think she would wait for us."

Dega had not looked around to see who had joined him. Now he did, and said with great admiration, "She is brave, is she not, Mother?"

Tihi chose her words with care. By no degree must she show disapproval. He might resent it. "Yes, Evelyn is brave. Brave is not always wise, though."

"In what way?"

"Look at her. She must know you care for her, yet she rides into danger with no thought for your feelings." Tihi smiled to blunt the blow.

"She thinks of all of us. Did you hear her about the war party?"

"I did. Which is why I would head west to the mountains. Instead, she takes us farther out into the prairie, farther from our valley, farther from safety."

Dega glanced over his shoulder at his father and his sisters.

"I worry for Teni and Miki," Tihi continued. "Remember what those white men almost did to Teni? A war party might do the same to them."

"Nate King says that rarely happens." But Dega was worried now, too.

"Rare does not mean never."

"I would give my life to prevent that from happening to them."

"You are a fine brother and son." Tihi adopted a lighthearted air. "But listen to us. Criticizing Evelyn when, as you say, she is only concerned for our welfare. She is a dear girl."

"Very dear."

"Your father thought the same of me when he was courting me. It was different for us, though, since we were both Nansusequa."

"Love is love," Dega said.

It was the first time her son openly used that word in referring to Evelyn King. Tihi realized she was broaching the subject at just the right time. "There are different kinds of love, my son. There is the love we share for Manitoa and all Manitoa provides. There is the love of a father and a mother for their children, and the love between brothers and sisters. Then there is the special love between a man and a woman. When they are of the same people or from the same tribe, they have much in common and their love is that much stronger. When they are not, their love is less than it could be."

"Less how, Mother?"

"The wife will want things her way, and the husband will want things his way. There are disagreements, arguments, fights."

"Not if they get along well."

"That is important, yes. But they cannot help being who they are. They cannot help how they were raised. They will not always agree, not as two people would who share the same beliefs."

"So are you saying it is wrong for a man and a woman to became husband and wife if they do not have a lot in common?"

Tihi gave him her sweetest smile. "I would never say that, Son. It is for the man and the woman to decide. Do they live in harmony with each other, as the Nansusequa believe they should, or do they argue and fight over whose way is best?"

Dega had a lot to ponder. He was still pondering when cottonwoods framed the horizon. He called to Evelyn.

Evelyn heard him, but she didn't slow. Since it was her idea to talk to the two warriors, she should take the risk of approaching them. She rode faster.

As she entered the trees, she spied two horses. She plastered a smile of greeting on her face and made sure to point her rifle at the ground so the warriors wouldn't get the wrong impression. She caught sight of the blue of a stream and heard the gurgling of water. Then she was in a clearing and saw a dead warrior on the ground in a pool of fresh blood and another warrior bound about the legs and a man who appeared to be a Negro or part Negro about to bash in the bound warrior's head with the stock of his rifle.

All this Evelyn took in at a glance. If she was surprised, so were they. No one moved. She thrust out her Hawken and thumbed back the hammer. "Hold it right there!"

Plenty Elk was astonished that the white woman would come to his aid. Yet that appeared to be exactly what she was doing. He expected the black man to fight. Instead, Rubicon whirled and was in among the cottonwoods in several long bounds.

Evelyn could have shot him. A light squeeze of the trigger and he was dead. But she refused to take a life unless she had no recourse. The black man looked back as the underbrush swallowed him. He grinned, as if he found it amusing that she hadn't done anything.

Dega arrived. He had seen the black man disappear into the vegetation, but he didn't go after him. His concern was for the girl he cared for.

Evelyn dismounted and went to the bound warrior. Drawing her knife, she slashed the rope around his legs, then stepped back.

Plenty Elk had been dazed by his friend's death. He had been dazed by the blow to his head. Now he was dazed again. He slowly sat up. "I do not know what to say."

Evelyn had heard Arapaho spoken a few times at Bent's Fort and elsewhere. It was unlike any other tongue. To confirm her hunch, she propped her rifle against her leg and signed, 'Question. You Arapaho?'

There was no end to the shocks Plenty Elk was enduring. To be saved by a white woman was amazing enough. For her to know sign talk was beyond belief. He wondered if he was unconscious and dreaming. One glance at Wolf's Tooth was enough to persuade him that it all was terribly real.

'Question. You Arapaho?' Evelyn signed again when she didn't get an answer.

'Yes.'

Waku and the rest of his family came hurrying through the trees and drew rein.

'I called Blue Flower,' Evelyn signed her Shoshone name. 'Grizzly Killer my father. You know him?'

Suddenly Plenty Elk understood. Yes, he had heard of the white Shoshone. A fierce fighter, by some accounts. It was said the man had taken a Shoshone woman as his blanket warmer and her tribe had adopted him. 'Question. Your mother Shoshone?' He asked because the white girl did not look as if she had a drop of Indian blood in her veins.

'Yes. My brother called Stalking Coyote. You know him?'

Plenty Elk had heard of her brother, too. Campfire stories had it that the brother was savage and had counted many coup. 'Yes.'

Evelyn reckoned that her father's and brother's reputations would work in her favor. Few men would dare their wrath by harming her. 'Question. Why your friend dead? Why black man try kill you?'

'Scalp hunter,' Plenty Elk signed.

Evelyn gave a start. If half the tales she'd heard

about scalpers were true, her friends were in dire peril. 'Question. How many scalp hunters? Where them now?'

Dega swung to the ground. He couldn't talk with his fingers like they were doing. He must wait for Evelyn to tell him what was being said. In the meantime, he would show he was friendly.

Plenty Elk was about to tell her about the ordeal he had been through when the green-garbed young man with her came over and held out his hand. His natural reaction was to suspect a trick, but the man seemed sincere about helping him. He took hold and let the other pull him to his feet.

Evelyn was about to introduce Waku and his family when she realized there weren't any signs for their names. The best she could do was point at each of them and say their names out loud.

Wakumassee. Tihikanima. Plenty Elk had never heard of names like theirs. He repeated them and was corrected when he mispronounced the older daughter's. He liked how she smiled at his mistake but not in a mocking manner.

Evelyn again asked about the scalp hunters. What she learned alarmed her. Turning to Waku, she translated, ending with, "We must leave before they get here. They won't care that you and your family are friendly. It won't matter that Miki is so young. All they'll think of is how much money your hair will bring."

Aghast, Waku nodded at his youngest. "They would kill her, too?" To slay another human being was bad enough. To kill a child was vile.

"They might." Evelyn would have herself to blame. The scalp hunters had no idea she and Waku's family were in the area until she went and butted in. Now the black would tell the rest and they would be after her and the Nansusequas like a pack of crazed wolves after sheep.

Plenty Elk coughed to get her attention. 'Question. What you do?'

'We run,' Evelyn signed. Fly like the wind was more like it, and the sooner they started, the better.

'You help me. I help you. I come with you. Together we fight scalp men.'

Evelyn hesitated. The Lord knew, they could use his help. But could she trust him? The Arapaho weren't as friendly as the Shoshones. Then again, they weren't as hostile as the Sioux. 'We happy you want fight for us.'

First they dug a shallow grave using broken tree branches and lowered Wolf's Tooth into the hole. They heaped dirt and branches and leaves on top to discourage scavengers.

Evelyn was grim as she climbed on the mare. They had gone from hunting buffalo to being the hunted, and it might well be that none of them would live to see the mountains ever again.

Chapter Seven

Venom was in no hurry. The two Dog Eaters who got away only thought they were safe. He would catch up to them presently and relieve them of their lives and their hair.

His company strung out behind him, Venom looked for the marks Rubicon made to guide them. At intervals the grass had been ripped out exposing the dirt. Each mark was about a yard long and half a foot wide and tapered in the direction they were to go.

Venom thought of the blood he had sucked from the scalp earlier and smacked his lips, wishing there had been more. Most folks didn't realize how delicious blood was. Back when he did it for the first time, when he was dying of thirst on the desert, he'd never imagined how much he would like it or how addicting it could be. He hadn't been joshing when he said that it was too bad blood wasn't sold in bottles like whiskey and ale.

Hooves thudded and he acquired a shadow at his elbow.

"What do you want, Logan?" Of all his men, Venom trusted Logan the least. Logan was snake-mean and as shifty as desert sands on a windy day, and Venom suspected he had aspirations.

"How long do you aim to wander all over this grassland looking for redskins before we head for New Mexico?"

"As long as I want. Do you have a problem with that?"

"You're the boss."

"That wasn't what I asked."

"Damn, you are a testy bastard." Logan laughed, but the sound rang hollow. "Have I ever complained?"

"You're too smart to gripe to my face."

"I wouldn't gripe behind your back, either. If I didn't like the way you were running this outfit, I'd say so."

"Or try to take over." Venom cocked an eyebrow. "What the hell difference does it make how long we take to get there?"

Logan rubbed the stubble on his chin. He looked at the clouds. Finally he said, "You remember that cantina in Santa Fe?"

"The one you spent all your time in? What about it?"

"You remember Maria?"

Venom snorted in amusement. Maria waited on the tables. She had long black hair and large moon eyes and more pounds on her than a heifer. She was so heavy she waddled when she walked. "What about her?"

"I've got plans for her."

Venom scowled. "You leave her be, you hear me? Too many people would miss her. There'd be folks nosing around, wondering where she got to. I learned my lesson with that Mex in Texas. Never kill anyone who will be missed."

"No one will ever suspect me."

"I just said no."

Now it was Logan who scowled. "You're not being fair. You get to drink blood all you want, but you won't let me do what I like?"

"What you like is to tie women down and do things that would get you hung in the States. What you like is to see them suffer. What you like is for them to beg and cry." Venom shook his head in disgust. "What you like is sick."

"Don't give me that. You've tortured. I've seen you."

"Now and then, sure. If someone makes me mad. Or if I need information. But I don't get the pleasure out of it that you do."

"It's not fair, I tell you."

Venom resented his tone. "I'll make it plain. You're not to touch Maria. Buck me on this and you will by-God regret it."

Logan was holding his rifle across his saddle. He started to raise it, but then lowered it again. "I don't like being threatened."

"I don't give a good damn what you do or don't like. You'll do as I damn well tell you."

"This is how you treat me when I've ridden with you longer than practically anyone?"

"This is how I treat you. Let me hear your word on Maria."

Logan swore and then growled, "I give you my word I won't touch the cow when we get to Santa Fe. Happy now?"

"If you need a female so much, we're bound to come across plenty of squaws. Do them."

"They're not as much fun. Most don't beg or cry." Logan went to rein around to fall back in line, and stiffened. "Look! Injuns!"

Venom whipped around in the saddle. To the northeast, so far away they were little more than vague shapes in the heat haze, were a lot of riders. Even at that distance it was obvious they weren't white.

Venom turned and pumped his right arm three times. It was a signal he had worked out. To a man his company promptly dismounted. Each gripped the bridle of his mount. Tugging and pulling, they coaxed their animals to the ground. Then they crouched with their rifles at the ready, their mounts now barriers against enemy lances and arrows.

Venom had a lot of tricks like this. Tricks that kept him and his men alive.

"Use your spyglass," Logan urged.

Venom disliked being told what to do, but he was about to take a look through the spyglass anyway. He opened his saddlebag, slid out the metal tube, and telescoped it as far it would go. Raising it to his eye, he studied the warriors. Lakotas, unless he missed his guess, or Sioux, as they were more commonly called.

"Well?" Potter nervously called out. "Can you tell who they are?"

Venom told him. "I count at least thirty. I think they're wearing war paint."

"You think?" Logan said.

"Have they spotted us?" Potter asked. "Folks say the Sioux are as fierce as Apaches. I sure don't want to tangle with any."

"You're a damn coward," Venom told him. A loyal coward who would do anything Venom wanted, no questions asked. "You can breathe easy. It appears they have no idea we're here."

"That's a lot of scalps," Tibbet remarked.

"Go ahead and try if you're that stupid." Venom

learned early on that in the scalping trade a man must know when to cut and when to fight shy and keep his own scalp.

"By my lonesome? No thank you. I like breathing as much as the next gent."

Venom kept watching through the spyglass. He didn't know what to make of it when the entire war party stopped. Then he saw one of the warriors point in his direction, and all the Sioux turned. "Damn!" He jerked the telescope down behind his horse.

"What's the matter?" Logan asked.

"I think one of them saw the sun reflect off the metal." Venom should have been more careful. He should have held his hat over the spyglass. It was the little mistakes that did a man in.

"Look again," Potter urged. "Maybe they're coming."

"Idiot." Venom could still see them, off in the haze. They hadn't moved. He glanced down the line to make sure none of his men was holding his rifle where the sun would gleam off the barrel as it had off the spyglass.

"They're movin' on!" one of the Kyler twins hollered.

That they were, continuing to the north, raising dust in their wake.

Venom stayed put until the war party was well gone. Then, rising, he gave the signal to stand.

"That was a close one," Potter said.

When they moved on, they did so warily. Venom sent the Kyler twins on ahead to ride point and sent Tibbet and Potter out to each side to cover their flanks. He deemed it unlikely the Lakotas would return, but it was better to be safe than dead.

In the excitement, Venom had forgotten to look for Rubicon's marks. When half an hour went by and none appeared he began to worry they had lost the trail. He was so preoccupied with finding it that when a rider reined in next to him, he glanced up in annoyance.

"What the hell do you want now?"

Logan answered, "It's not our day."

"Care to explain, or am I supposed to figure it out for myself?"

Extending an arm to the southwest, Logan said, "I haven't seen one of those critters this far out in a coon's age."

Venom sensed what he would see before he turned. A quarter of a mile off, lumbering on all fours, was a creature as massive as a buffalo but ten times as dangerous, and as difficult to kill as anything. "Hell."

A huge grizzly was bound who-knew-where. The hump, the tree-trunk legs, the huge head with jaws that could crush bone at a bite—the last thing Venom wanted was to have it attack.

"It hasn't seen us yet."

"It's the nose we have to worry about." Venom licked the tip of his finger and raised it over his head. The breeze was blowing from west to east—from the bear to them. They were safe so long as the wind didn't shift. One whiff of their scent and the grizzly might decide to fill its belly.

"That hide would fetch a good price at Bent's Fort."

"Scalps fetch more." Plus, Venom didn't intend to stop at Bent's. The last time they had, on their way to St. Louis, Ceran St. Vrain, who ran the place along with the Bent brothers, treated them as if they had the plague. St. Vrain had a low opinion of scalp men, as he'd made clear when he cornered Venom in the stable.

"I'd like a word with you, if you don't mind."

Venom had been honing his knife. "I suppose if I do, you'll have your word anyway?"

"I'm serving notice. You would be well advised to heed, or the consequences will be severe."

"Damn, you talk pretty," Venom taunted, but his barb had no effect on the haughty master of the trading post.

"These grounds are a safe haven for anyone who desires to visit. That applies to red and white alike."

Venom knew that. Tribes at war put aside their animosity when they visited Bent's or they were banned from trading, and no tribe wanted that, not when Bent's Fort was the only place within a thousand miles where they could trade for everything from rifles to steel knives to pots and pans. "So?"

"So I'm aware of how you earn your despicable livelihood, Mr. Venom. I don't approve, but then each man to his own affairs."

"My sentiments exactly."

"However"—St. Vrain leaned down, his face as hard as iron—"there will be no taking the scalp of any Indian who visits our post. Not here, not for fifty miles around."

"Fifty miles?" Venom bristled. "Who do you think you are, God Almighty? You have the right to tell me what not to do when I'm within these walls, but you sure as hell don't have the right to tell me what to do fifty miles from here. You don't own the prairie."

"True," St. Vrain conceded. "But all I have to do is snap my fingers and I'll have twenty armed men ready to enforce my edict, along with a large number of our Indian friends."

"Are you threatening me?"

"Yes."

The man's bluntness rankled. Venom wasn't used to being treated as if he was of no account. "I should gut you where you stand."

"You won't find it easy. And keep in mind that if you

try, you and your cutthroats won't make it out the gate alive."

The hell of it was, Venom was forced to back down. St. Vrain's men were a salty bunch, and the Indians all thought highly of him. "Listen. I'm not after scalps. We're here to buy grub and tobacco and whatnot. Then we'll be on our way."

St. Vrain turned to go. "Remember what I told you about the fifty-mile limit. Word will get back to me if you don't heed. You might think you can lift a few scalps and get clean away, but how long would you last with a five-hundred-dollar bounty on your own hair?"

"You wouldn't."

"Try me and find out." St. Vrain walked to the stable door and turned. "Some of us, Mr. Venom, happen to like the Indians. We regard them as human beings. One of my partners, William Bent, is married to a Cheyenne. All he has to do is get word to them and every warrior in the tribe will descend upon you and do what should have been done years ago."

On that sour note, their talk had ended. Just thinking about it left a bitter taste in Venom's mouth.

A shout brought him out of his reverie.

"Here come the Kyler twins! And Rubicon is with them!"

To say Venom was surprised was an understatement. He contained his anger as the rest of his men converged, and when the twins and the black man drew rein, he jabbed a finger at Rubicon. "What the hell are you doing here? I thought I told you to track those Arapaho bucks."

"I did," Rubicon said, his face alight with suppressed excitement. "I killed one and took his hair and was saving the other one for you, like you wanted. But then some others came along."

"Other Arapahos?"

"No. Indians, the likes of which I've never seen, all of them wearing green buckskins."

"The deuce you say."

"A whole family, from what I could make out, five in all."

"This gets more interesting by the moment."

"There's a mother and a couple of girls. One of them is almost full grown and as pretty as can be."

"Well, now." Venom grinned.

"There's more. I've saved the best for last."

"Spit it out, damn you. What could be better than five scalps and some fun, besides?"

"There's a white girl with them."

Venom's grin widened. "Did you hear him, boys? Christmas has come early this year."

Chapter Eight

They headed west as fast they could without riding their horses into the ground. To the west were the mountains. To the west was King Valley and safety. Or so Evelyn hoped. The problem was getting there. Even riding hard, it would take seven to eight days to reach the foothills and another ten days to reach home.

It was simply too far.

Evelyn realized that if the scalp hunters came after them, they were as good as caught. Waku and his family had never sat on a horse until recently. They were middling riders, and their lack of experience would do them in. She could see the strain beginning to tell already, and they hadn't been underway more than a few hours. Dega was doing well enough, but then he'd done a lot of riding with her. Teni did pretty well, too, but Tihi and the youngest, Miki, and Waku, himself, had yet to learn how to sit a horse so that a long, hard ride didn't set their leg muscles to cramping and their insides to feeling as if they had been tossed around in a tornado.

Plenty Elk rode the best of them all. He impressed Evelyn. She evidently impressed him, too, because at one point, when they stopped to rest, he signed that she was a good rider. She thanked him for the compliment and turned to see Dega watching, his expression peculiar.

They pushed on until twilight and made camp in a basin where the glow of their fire wouldn't give them away and they were sheltered from the night wind. Thanks to their water skin and plenty of jerky and pemmican they didn't want for drink or food.

The young Arapaho got the fire going, using buffalo droppings for fuel. She vividly remembered the time her mother took her to visit the Shoshones and her uncle, Touch the Clouds, gathered buffalo chips for a fire. She'd refused to sit near it because she was sure the stink would make her sick. Her mother and her uncle humored her, but when the cold got to her, she came and sat with them, and discovered, to her amazement, that the odor was more like that of a musty old rug than the foul reek she'd expected.

Now, Evelyn hunkered and held her hands out to the dancing flames. She liked the warmth on her palms.

Across from her, Waku moved his legs and winced.

"You're hurting, aren't you?"

"Some, yes," Waku acknowledged.

"You'll hurt worse tomorrow night," Evelyn predicted. "You're just not used to the kind of riding we have to do."

Waku stretched and winced again. "Are you sure they will come, these scalp men?"

"My pa told me about scalp hunters. He says there's not a shred of virtue in any of them. They kill a person and don't bat an eye. Old, young, male, female, human life means nothing. All they care about is money." Evelyn listened to the yip of a coyote. "I don't know how much they get for a scalp.

But you can bet it's enough to make what they do worth it to them, even with the risks. You and your family are money in their pokes. So, yes, I think they'll come after us."

Waku gazed at his loved ones. Once again they were in danger. He missed the old times, before the massacre, before they were forced to flee, back when his world was peaceful and orderly and his family wasn't constantly in danger.

Dega was listening intently. "These scalp men come, we fight." He would die rather than let Evelyn or his family be harmed.

Evelyn wanted to avoid a clash if she could help it. They were bound to be outnumbered. The scalp hunters would be better armed, too, with rifles and pistols for every man.

Resting her chin on her knees, Evelyn wrapped her arms around her legs and contemplated how in God's name she could save her friends. It seemed hopeless. Here they were, surrounded by miles and miles of open prairie. There was nowhere to hide. There was no way to conceal their trail. The scalp hunters would track them and kill them, and that would be that.

For a few moments Evelyn hung on the cusp of despair. But then something her pa had been drumming into her since she was a sprout took root. "Never give up," he'd often said. "Kings aren't quitters. When the going gets tough, we do what we have to."

Evelyn had more of her pa in her than she imagined. She refused to give up. She refused to let the scalp hunters kill her friends. But how to stop them when they were seasoned slayers while she was what some would call a slip of a girl and her friends were the most peaceable people on earth?

As her pa would say, where there was a will, there was a way.

Evelyn raised her head and peered into the night. Yes, they were in the middle of the prairie, but the prairie didn't lack for cover. There were rolling hills and washes and gullies and tracts of woodland. There were streams and a few rivers. They must use the land to its best advantage.

Dega had been noting her every expression, and at the look on her face he said, "Evelyn?"

"Yes?"

"What you think about?"

"How to win?"

"Win?" Dega recalled that to win was the purpose of a game called checkers she had been trying to teach him.

"How to keep you and your family breathing. We have to make it cost the scalp hunters more than you are worth so they'll give up and leave us be." Evelyn gnawed her lower lip. "Either that, or we have to kill every last one of the buzzards."

"Scalp men are birds?"

Evelyn laughed. She had to remember that he took her every word literally. "Not the way you mean, no. When a white says someone is a buzzard, it means they are no account."

Dega tried to make sense of it. "Buzzard is same as vulture, yes?"

"Yes."

"Vultures eat dead things. That what they do. That their . . ." Dega struggled for the right white word. ". . . purpose." He beamed, pleased with himself.

"Yes, that's true, too."

"How that be bad?"

"It isn't. It's the nature of things."

"Then how scalp hunters same as vultures?"

Evelyn wrestled with her wits to get it across. "A lot of whites don't like buzzards. Same as they don't like skunks. So when they don't like someone, whites call that person a buzzard or a polecat."

"Why whites no like vultures?"

"Because they eat carrion. Sorry, they eat the flesh of dead things."

"But that what vultures do."

"As you said, it's their purpose, yes."

Dega scrunched up his face in annoyance at his failure to understand. "So white people not like vulture to be vulture?"

"It's the eating of dead things. The notion makes white people sick to their stomachs. Besides which, buzzards are ugly as sin."

Dega was on the verge of a headache. Vultures couldn't help doing what they did. It was their nature. As for being ugly, all living things were of Manitoa, each according to their own kind, and had a beauty in their own right. He'd always thought that a vulture in flight was a noble sight. Now Evelyn was saying whites thought vultures were ugly. "I be a poor white."

"How's that again?"

"Whites not think like Nansusequa. Whites think white. I try but not think same."

"Well, of course, silly," Evelyn said. "You have to be you. Just as I have to be me. That doesn't mean we can't have a meeting of the minds, now does it?"

Dega was ready to scream from confusion. She had just asked him a question and he had no idea what she had asked. She was right that he had to be him, but then, who else would he be? And she was right that she had to be her, but if she were someone else, she wouldn't be Evelyn. And if he was him and she was her, how were their minds to meet? He pressed his palms to his temple.

"Something the matter?"

"My head hurt from too much think."

"You try too hard. Things will come to you naturally if you let them. All in good time, as us whites like to say."

Dega refused to give up. "How minds meet?"

"Oh. When two people who don't see eye to eye work things out so they do see eye to eye, we call that a meeting of the minds."

His despair mounting, Dega almost groaned out loud. Somehow they had gone from minds to eyes and back again. Here he wanted her to be proud of how well he talked, but again and again he became mired in confusion. Part of the problem was that he couldn't grasp the nuances of the white tongue.

"Don't look so glum. You're doing fine. My pa says that when he first met my ma, they had to communicate by sign for the longest time. She picked up his tongue quick, but he had to work hard at learning Shoshone."

The mention of sign caused Dega to glance at the Arapaho, who was staring sadly into the flames. Dega imagined he was thinking of the friends he had lost. Dega should feel sympathy, but he felt something else. "Think maybe I learn sign talk quick."

"I'll teach you if you want, but it might be better to stick with English until you get that down."

Dega looked across the fire, into her eyes. "You like him?"

"Who?"

Dega nodded at the Arapaho.

"He's nice enough," Evelyn allowed. She remembered the look Dega had given her earlier, and her intuition flared. "Why do you ask? You're not jealous, are you?"

"What be jealous?"

Evelyn hesitated. He might take it the wrong way. "Jealous is when you like someone and don't want anyone else to like them."

"No. I not jealous." Dega wasn't being honest. He had felt a twinge of . . . something . . . when she was signing to Plenty Elk. Something he never felt before, something raw and hot and disturbing.

"Oh." Evelyn was disappointed.

Waku had been listening with keen interest without being obvious he was listening. His wife's comments had kindled his curiosity. As near as he could make out, though, his son and Evelyn King did not act as he and Tihi did when they courted. If they were in love, they were hiding it, even from themselves. Yet there was no denying the looks they gave each other, usually when the other wasn't looking. As he saw it, it would be a good while before they grew close enough to contemplate sharing the same lodge—his, or any other.

From out of the dark came a grunt.

Evelyn leaped to her feet with her Hawken in her hands. "That was a bear." She hoped a black bear and not a grizzly. The latter was much more likely to attack.

Dega rose, too, and notched an arrow to his bow. "Fire keep bear away."

"Not a griz. Not if it's hungry enough."

Everyone listened and waited in tense expectation. The grunt was repeated, only closer.

Turning, Evelyn saw a pair of glowing eyes. They were almost on a level with her own. "Don't anyone do anything rash," she whispered. "Dega, translate for your mother and sisters."

Eager to please her, Dega did.

Little Miki edged over to Tihi and clasped her arm. "Mother?"

"Be still and it will go away."

Plenty Elk stood and faced the bear. Raising his arms above his head, he let out with a loud screech.

Evelyn jerked the Hawken to her shoulder. She had her thumb on the hammer, ready to curl it back, but the bear wheeled and melted into the darkness with a parting snort. Forgetting herself, she said to the young warrior, "That was a darned fool stunt. You could have gotten us killed."

Plenty Elk lowered his arms. 'Question. What you speak?'

Leaning the Hawken against her leg, Evelyn signed, 'You maybe make bear mad. Bear attack.'

'Bear no like war cry. Bear always go.'

Not always, but Evelyn let it drop. She added chips to the fire so the flames blazed brighter, then scanned the night for glowing eyes. Only when she was convinced the monster had left did she sit back down, cross-legged, with the Hawken in her lap. She wouldn't be able to sleep for hours now. "Stupid bear," she muttered.

"Why people no be nice?" Dega asked.

Coming as it did out of the blue, the question mystified Evelyn. "Where did that come from?"

"Nice come from heart."

"No, I mean, why did you ask?"

"White men who kill my people. Scalp men who take hair for money. Other bad men. Why people no be nice?"

"You're asking me?"

"I just do ask."

Evelyn chuckled. "I've wondered the same thing since I was knee-high to a grasshopper. The answer

I came up with is that some people are naturally nice and some aren't."

"That all?"

"What more do you need?"

"Scalp men have hearts with no nice."

"I couldn't have put it better, myself. So when the time comes, don't hold back. It will be them or us."

Dega stared at his mother and father and sisters. "I no want it be us." He smiled. "I no want it be you."

Evelyn King grew warm all over.

Chapter Nine

The scalp hunters were in good spirits. The scent of prey was in the wind and the only thing they liked more than the hunt was spending the money they made from scalping the hunted.

Venom had sent Rubicon on ahead to track. As usual, his men were strung out behind him in a line. They raised less dust that way. When one of his men came up beside him he didn't look to see who it was. He knew. "Keep this up and I'll get good and mad."

"It's about the girl," Logan said.

"Which girl? There are two red and one white."

"The white girl," Logan amended. He hesitated, cleared his throat, and declared, "I want her."

"You haven't even set eyes on her yet."

"I still want her."

"Do you, now?" Venom didn't keep the scorn out of his voice. "You must be confused. The rule has always been that each of us gets to keep the scalps of the redskins we kill. When it comes to other spoils, it's share and share alike."

"You can make an exception if you want."

"I don't want," Venom said.

Logan frowned and shifted in his saddle. "Damn

it. Why not? I'll pay the others a share of my scalp money if that's what will persuade you."

"You'd do that?"

"I need a woman. I need a woman bad. You wouldn't understand because you don't get the itch like I do."

"What else?" Venom prompted.

"How do you mean?"

Venom almost struck him. "You must take me for a fool. What's the real reason you want this white girl when you could have the Injun girls or their mother?"

Logan looked away. "You think you have me figured out."

"Go annoy someone else." Venom went to lift his reins.

"All right, all right." Logan swore, then said, "I want her because she's white. I don't often get to do white girls, not how I like to do them, anyhow. It'd get me strung up faster than anything."

"So you reckon to have this white girl all to yourself? Take your sweet time doing those awful things you do?"

"You're a fine one to talk."

Venom enjoyed baiting him. "The answer is still no."

Logan scowled and opened his mouth but closed it again and visibly controlled himself. "I'm asking you nice."

"Are you now?" Venom smirked. "Have I ever told you how I feel about *nice*? Nice is for the weak. Nice is for the puny. Nice is for those too soft to take what they want. So they go around being nice to everybody and hope to get it that way."

"Damn it all."

"I'm not finished. Nice is for farmers and town

folk and those who have blinders on. They think the world is a nice place to live. They think God is nice and they should be the same. Nice is stupid."

"Rub my nose in it, why don't you?"

Venom shook his head. "You're not paying attention. This isn't just about you. It's about *nice*. Nice people make me sick to my stomach because the world isn't nice. It's hard and cruel and doesn't give a damn whether people live or die. As for the Almighty, if there is one, he can't be all that nice if he lets you and me do the things we do."

"You're no churchgoer, that's for sure."

"Now, now. Don't get personal. How many times must I tell you? This is about nice. You sit there and you say that you're asking me nice. Well, you can take your *nice* and shove it up your ass. That's where it belongs."

"So your answer is still no?"

"You catch on quick." Venom figured that was the end of it, but Logan had more to say.

"What if I pay you and just you? All the money I make this time?"

"That wouldn't be fair to the others. Some of them are bound to want to have her."

Logan brightened. "What if I pay you to let me have her after they're done with her?"

Before Venom could respond, Potter called out from down the line.

"Look to the north!"

Everyone did. Coils of gray smoke were writhing skyward about a mile off. Not just one coil but three.

Venom drew rein. "Redskins wouldn't be so stupid as to give themselves away like that."

"It must be white men," Logan agreed.

"Let's go have a look-see. It could be cavalry. The

army hardly ever gets out this far, but if it's a patrol it's best we find out which way they're heading so we don't run into them later." Venom rose in the stirrups and swept his arm to the north then reined toward the smoke.

Logan stayed at his side. "You haven't answered me about the white girl. Can I have her after the rest have a turn? I'll pay you for the privilege."

"I want a million dollars."

"Be serious."

"You just don't know when to quit," Venom said coldly. "My answer now is the same as it was when you first asked. Now get back in line, and send the Kyler twins up here." When there was potential trouble or killing to be done, Venom relied on the Kylers. The pair had a natural knack for death dealing, just like some folks had a knack for arithmetic or for painting or music. Presently they joined him, each holding his rifle across his saddle with his thumb on the hammer and finger on the trigger. They were always primed, these two.

"What's it to be then, boss?" asked the one on his right.

For the life of him, Venom couldn't tell them apart. One was called Seph and the other was Jeph, but they were so alike it was impossible to say who was who. "I don't know yet. If it's the army, we play at being sociable. We'll tell them we're buffalo hunters."

"Reckon they'll believe it?" asked the twin on the left.

"They might know about those Pawnees we killed," said the other.

"It's not a crime to kill Injuns. But send word back down the line for everyone to keep their scalps in their saddlebags."

"I'll do it," said the twin on the right, and reined around.

"What was Logan talkin' to you about?" inquired the Kyler who was still there.

Venom glanced at him sharply. The twins tended to keep to themselves and rarely poked their noses into what anyone else did. "What do you care?"

"Seph and me think he was askin' you about the white girl, and we don't like it much."

About to answer, Venom noticed that Jeph's ear had a small nick out of it. Apparently he'd been cut once. "I'll be damned."

"What?"

"I finally found a way to tell you two peas apart." Venom chuckled, then sobered. "Now what's this about the white girl?"

"Seph and me don't cotton to the notion of white girls bein' hurt. Redskins, greasers, darkies, it don't matter with them. White girls it does."

"How come you never said anything before? Don't tell me Seph and you grew scruples all of a sudden."

"Rubicon was sayin' as how this one is real pretty."

"Oh. So it's all right for Logan to carve up the ugly ones but not the good-looking ones."

"White is white. We held our tongues before because you let him and you're the boss. But it festered some, and we have to speak our piece."

"I'm glad you came to me and didn't confront him." Venom could see Logan getting riled and the Kylers making worm food of him. Logan was tough, but when it came to being deadly the twins had him beat all hollow.

The smoke from the campfires continued to writhe into the sky. Venom took out his spyglass.

He counted ten wagons drawn up in a circle near a tract of trees. They were prairie schooners, red and blue with canvas tops. Men with rifles were herding oxen toward the trees, possibly to let them drink at a spring. "Unless I miss my guess it's a bull train."

"Freighters?" Jeph said. "They must be on their way to Santa Fe."

"Could be."

Through the spyglass Venom saw a man posted outside the wagons cup a hand to his mouth and point in their direction. Others came out of the circle, each bristling with weapons. "Remember to smile and be nice." He grinned at his use of the word.

A thick man with powerful shoulders came to the front and planted his stout legs. He put his hands on a pair of pistols wedged under a brown belt and regarded them with the eyes of a wolf. His chin was covered with stubble and he had a short-brimmed hat pushed back on a brown thatch of hair. "What do you want?" he demanded as Venom drew rein.

"We saw your smoke and thought maybe you might have coffee on."

"Indeed we do, but we're not inclined to share. If it's a warm welcome you're looking for, find yourself a pilgrim train."

Venom saw why the freighters had stopped; one of the wagons had a busted wheel. A pair of brawny freight men had used a jack to raise the bed and were busy replacing broken spokes. "You're not very neighborly, friend."

"No, I'm not. Nor am I your friend." The man nodded at the circle. "This is my train. I'm the captain, Jeremiah Blunt. You will notice there are twenty-two of us and only eight of you. If any of you so much as lifts a gun, you will all die in your saddles."

"Damn, you're a mean cuss," Venom said with genuine respect.

"I've never lost a wagon," Jeremiah Blunt declared. "Never lost a man, either. I don't intend to start now."

"All we wanted was to share your fire and some coffee."

"I don't make a habit of repeating myself, but your ears must be plugged with wax. Our coffee is ours. Our fires are ours. You have come as close as you are going to and now you will leave."

"I can see you treating redskins this way, but we're white."

"You say that as if skin matters. It doesn't."

Venom's admiration was changing to anger. "I don't like being treated as if I'm no account."

"Do I look as if I care what you like?"

"We're buffalo hunters." Venom tried a new tack. "We thought you might have seen—" He got no further.

Blunt cut him off. "When trees grow fur."

"What's that?"

"You're no more hide hunters than I am." Blunt sniffed a few times. "You don't have the stink."

"You can tell what a man does by how he smells?" Venom sarcastically asked.

"Some, yes. A miner smells of the dust and the earth. A cowhand smells of horses and cows. Buffalo hunters smell of blood and gore. Your stink is different. You stink of death."

It was such a remarkable statement that Venom was left speechless for one of the few times in his entire life.

"I don't know what you men are and I don't care. All I care about is my train. Be on your way and don't come anywhere near us, or the next time we'll shoot you on sight."

"You're awful rude."

Blunt drew a pistol and pointed it at Venom. The click of the hammer was ominously loud. "Talking to you is like talking to an infant. Make yourselves scarce or we'll make you dead."

The other freighters raised rifles and pistols.

Venom was fit to explode. It was bad enough to be treated this way. It was worse that his men had to see him humiliated. All he'd wanted was to jaw a spell, maybe find out if the freighters had come across Indian sign. He reined around but paused to say, "I won't forget this. I won't forget how you've treated us for no reason."

"Mister, I have all the reason in the world," Blunt responded, the pistol rock-steady in his hand. "The freight in those wagons has been entrusted to me. Those who hired me know I'll get it where it has to go. Neither Indians nor brigands nor Nature itself will stay me in my course."

Potter cleared his throat. "Why are we wasting our time with this cantankerous bastard when there's that white girl and her friends to find?"

Jeremiah Blunt glanced sharply at him.

Venom swiveled to give Potter a look that made him recoil as if he'd been hit. Swearing under his breath, Venom turned back to the freight captain. "Thanks for nothing, you grumpy goat." He rode off and didn't look back. He didn't want his men to see how mad he was. He must always give the impression he was made of iron. Any hint of weakness, and one of them might take it into their head to challenge his leadership. Logan, for instance.

Suddenly the Kyler twins were on both sides of him.

"What the hell do you two want?"

"We can fix him for you. One shot is all it would take."

Venom glanced at their ears. "He's not worth the bother, Jeph. His men might come after us, and like Potter said, we have that white girl and her Injun friends to think of."

"I'd never let anyone talk to me the way Blunt did to you," Seph remarked.

"No, you'd have shot him and gotten the rest of us killed." Venom was about to add that they should fall back in line when the rest of his men came up alongside.

"Say the word, boss," Potter said.

"You're lunkheads, the whole bunch of you."

"We could wait until tonight and jump them," Potter persisted.

"Maybe lose half of us, and for what?" Venom said gruffly. "To punish them for their insult? Then what? We sell their freight? Because we sure as hell can't turn in their scalps for bounty money. Hardly any of them had hair dark enough or long enough to be mistook for Injun hair."

Logan snorted in what could only be contempt. "If it'd been me the bastard treated that way, I wouldn't slink off with my tail between my legs."

Venon reined up so abruptly that Calvert, who was behind him, nearly rode into his horse. Everyone else also came to a stop. "What did you just say?"

"A man has to stand up for himself or he's not much of a man."

"You're suggesting I'm yellow?"

"What? No. You make an insult where none is intended."

"Now I'm stupid as well as yellow."

"Damn it," Logan said. "Stop putting words in my mouth. I don't blame you for being angry. That wagon boss made you eat crow. But don't take it out on me. Go back there and knock his teeth in."

"I have a better idea." Venom drew his pistol and shot him.

Chapter Ten

The hard part was not knowing when the scalp hunters would catch up. It was like sour food in the pit of Evelyn' s stomach, an ache that wouldn't go away. The others were worried, too. She could see it in their faces. Except for Plenty Elk. He didn't seem worried at all. Maybe it was the deaths of his friends. He acted eager for a fight, as if he had something to prove. Whatever his reasons, Evelyn was glad he was there.

Waku and his family weren't fighters. The Nansusequa had been a peaceful tribe. They fought only when provoked. From what Evelyn could gather, most eastern tribes didn't esteem counting coup as highly as tribes west of the Mississippi River. Why that should be was another of life's many mysteries.

All morning they rode hard. When the sun was at its zenith, they stopped to rest their lathered mounts.

Evelyn passed out pemmican. She gave a piece to Plenty Elk and he signed his thanks. He had more to sign.

'Scalp men catch us tomorrow.'

'No today?'

'They have far ride where black man kill my friend. They have far ride here.'

Evelyn wasn't so sure. The scalp hunters would push hard, too. 'Maybe when sun go down.'

'Question. White men fight night?'

'Yes.' Evelyn was aware many tribes usually only waged war during the day. Some whites believed it was due to a superstitious taboo. Common sense was the real reason. Fighting in the dark, when a person could hardly see, was an invite to an early grave.

'Question. You have husband?'

Evelyn was startled. It had been her experience that Indian men, especially Indian men her age, only asked that question when they had designs in that direction. 'I have no mate,' she signed.

'You beautiful.'

'Thank you.'

'You smell good.'

Evelyn was flabbergasted. Here they were, fleeing for their lives from a pack of demons in human guise, and this young warrior was trying to court her. 'You smell my sweat,' she signed.

'Sweat smell good,' Plenty Elk persisted.

Men, Evelyn decided, were too ridiculous for words. She smiled and went over to Dega and gave him a piece of pemmican from the beaded parfleche her mother had made.

"What you two hand talk about?" Dega asked.

"Nothing much."

Dega had been watching them closely, and he was sure it was more than nothing. He had seen her face, seen how she reacted to something the Arapaho warrior signed. "Him have big ears."

"Excuse me?"

Dega touched one of his own ears to emphasize how much smaller his were. "His ears too much big. Look funny."

"I thought the Nansusequa don't judge people by how they look but by how they are inside," Evelyn reminded him.

"We do." Dega felt it necessary to justify his lapse. "I not judge his ears. I just say they big."

"He can't help how he was born."

That she would defend the Arapaho worried Dega considerably. "You like his ears more or my ears more?"

"Ears are ears."

"Please. Which ears best?"

Was it her imagination, Evelyn asked herself, or was Dega jealous? "Mountain lion ears are sharpest," she answered, and went over to Teni. The older girl took a piece of pemmican and thanked her in the Nansusequa tongue.

Dega squatted and held a counsel with himself. Perhaps it was time he told Evelyn how he felt. Until now he had hidden his true feelings, afraid that if he revealed them, she would want nothing more to do with him.

Evelyn faced east and shielded her eyes with her hand. The distant haze was unbroken save by a flock of birds in flight. She turned and nearly bumped into Waku, who had come up behind her. "Goodness. Scare a person, why don't you?"

"Sorry."

"No need to apologize. I'm jumpy."

"No sign of the scalp men yet." Waku had been anxiously watching their back trail all morning.

"Not yet, no." Evelyn had been thinking, and she had an idea. For it to work, she needed to know something. "Tell me. Will your family kill if they have to?"

"My son and me kill if bad men catch us," Waku promised.

"No, not just you two," Evelyn clarified. "What

about Tihikanima and Teni and little Miki? Have they ever killed?"

"They are women. They are not warriors." Waku liked the Kings, liked them dearly, but they were too prone to violence. In that regard they were no different from the tribes of the region, who waged war for the sheer excitement. An attitude that ran contrary to all he believed. The Nansusequa valued peace above all else.

"Shoshone women will kill to defend their village. The same with the Sioux and the Crows and the Blackfeet," Evelyn said. "Will your wife and daughters do the same?"

It hit Waku, then, what she was suggesting. "You want them to help kill the scalp men?"

"We could ambush the whole bunch," Evelyn proposed. "Plenty Elk says there are nine of them. Well, there are seven of us. I could give one of my pistols to your wife and another to Teni. You and Dega both have bows. So does Plenty Elk. I have my rifle. If we did it right, if we let them come up close so we couldn't miss, we could drop six of them before they got off a shot. That would leave three for us to deal with."

Waku was amazed she would propose subjecting his wife and daughters to such terror. "Not Tihi, Teni and Miki."

"I can teach Tihi and Teni to shoot the pistols. It's no feat at all if your target is near enough. You just point and squeeze."

"No."

"Why not? It's our best chance of ending this and saving all our lives. The scalp hunters won't ride into an ambush twice."

"Not my wife and daughters."

"You don't want them to kill even when they might be killed? Where's the logic in that?"

"You do not understand," Waku said.

"Enlighten me." Evelyn was convinced an ambush would work but only once. They must make it count. They must slay as many scalp hunters as they could with their first volley of lead and arrows.

"You are a white girl . . ."

"I'm half Indian," Evelyn reminded him.

"Your mother is Indian, yes. But you do not look like her. You look like your father. You are more white than Indian."

"What does that have to do with anything?"

"Tihikanima and Tenikawaku and Mikikawaku are Nansusequa. They live the Nansusequa way. We are raised to not take life unless we must."

"We have to now, or we're goners."

Waku sighed. There were times when it seemed that the white solution to every conflict was to kill. His people had been wiped out by whites who craved their land, and the only way those whites could think of to get it was to kill every last Nansusequa. That the Nansusequa wouldn't have given the land up under any circumstance was beside the point.

Waku had noticed the same trait in his new white friends, to a greater or lesser degree. Zach King, Evelyn's brother, was a notorious manslayer. Shakespeare McNair, mentor to her father, had no qualms about slaying an enemy. As for Nate King, he had done his share, but always reluctantly, always when there was no other recourse.

Of all the whites Waku ever met, he respected Nate King the most. Nate's outlook was a lot like his own. It was to be regretted that more people, red and white, didn't share their view. Many fewer lives would be lost.

"Tell me, then," Evelyn prompted. "What do *you*

want to do? How do you want to deal with the scalp men?"

Waku had to think to remember the right word. "Flee."

"You want to run?"

"If run is the same as flee, yes."

Now it was Evelyn who sighed. "Do you realize how far we are from the foothills? What chance do you think we have of reaching them alive with the scalp men after us every foot of the way?"

"We must try."

To Evelyn it was lunacy. The scalp hunters were bound to overtake them. "When they catch us, as they surely will, what will you and your family do then? Turn and fight?"

"If they catch us, yes."

Evelyn had been raised to respect her elders. Her inclination was to bow to his wishes. Giving in, though, could cost them to pay too high a price for his ideal.

"My family will run," Waku declared. "We will not fight if we can help it."

Evelyn's exasperation knew no bounds. Tihi, Teni and even Dega would do as Waku told them. To try to talk them into bucking him would be a waste of her breath. The only one Evelyn could count on to side with her was Plenty Elk, and the two of them alone stood no chance at all against nine hardened cutthroats. "You're making a mistake."

"It will not be my first."

Disappointed, Evelyn went off by herself a dozen yards, tucked her legs under her, and gloomily munched on a piece of pemmican. When a shadow fell across her she sensed who it was before he spoke.

"You look much sad."

"Your pa won't listen to reason."

Dega sat across from her. "I see you talk to him. I see your face. I come make you smile."

"Tucking our tails between our legs isn't how we should deal with this. When your back is to the wall you bite and scratch."

"Tuck tails?"

"It means to run. That's what your pa wants to do. Run until they're on top of us. But unless we whittle down the odds first, I'm afraid we'll all be bald before the week is out." Evelyn smiled thinly at her poor joke.

Dega repeated her statements in his head. He understood the running part and the bald part but the whittling part was a puzzle. To whittle had to do with carving wood with a knife. Shakespeare Mc-Nair liked to whittle. How that had anything to do with the scalp hunters was beyond him. He fished for more information by saying, "You think whittle good idea?"

"It makes sense, doesn't it, to get in the first licks? Catch them with their guard down. Maybe make half of them goners before they know what hit them."

Once again Dega wrestled with her meaning. Licking was what a person did with their tongue, but she certainly couldn't be suggesting they lick the scalp hunters. As for goners, that sounded a lot like gone, and gone was when someone went away. So she must be saying that she would like half the scalp hunters to go away. But where? And what was to stop them from coming back? He began to despair of ever learning the white tongue.

"I wish my pa was here. Or Zach. They're better at this sort of thing than I am."

"You girl."

"Thank goodness. To tell you the truth, I never

could stand the bloodshed. Ever since I was old enough to remember, our family has had to fight for survival. Fight against hostile Indians, against white scoundrels, against wild beasts, against nature." Evelyn paused. "When I was small, I'd get down on my knees next to my bed at night and pray that God would let us get through the next day without something or someone trying to kill us. Silly, huh?"

"Smart."

"It's not like this back East. You can go your whole life long and no one ever lifts a finger against you. There isn't a bear over every mountain or a war party over every hill. A body can go about their business in perfect peace." Evelyn bit off more pemmican. "That's partly why I wanted to move back there for so long. I was sick and tired of always having to look over my shoulder. It grates on the nerves."

Dega had noticed that while the mountains were wonderlands of beauty, perils lurked in the shadows. He couldn't go anywhere, even in King Valley, unless he was armed.

"Here I wanted this trip to be fun," Evelyn said quietly. "We'd shoot a buff and peel the hide and take enough meat back to last your family a couple of months or more. I never counted on anything like this."

Another shadow fell across her. This time it was Plenty Elk. He pointed to the east.

Evelyn looked and didn't see anything. Only the grass and the sky and the summer haze. Then her eyes narrowed. A speck had appeared, a speck in motion, miles away yet but there was no mistaking the fact it was smack on their back trail. "Their tracker," she guessed.

"The black man, you think?" Dega asked.

Evelyn nodded and stood. "The others can't be far

behind. We'll have to ride like the wind to stay ahead of them."

"I tell my family," Dega said.

Plenty Elk signed, 'Question. You want do with black man?'

There was no sign for "what." Evelyn had to fill it in mentally. She responded with, 'Question. You want do?'

Plenty Elk mimicked drawing his bowstring and releasing an arrow.

'You me think same,' Evelyn signed, and grinned.

Chapter Eleven

Rubicon liked being a scalper. He got to track, and tracking was something he was good at. He also got to kill Indians, of whom he was not all that fond.

Rubicon had been born and raised in Rhode Island. Most people assumed he was a former slave or the son of a slave, but he was neither.

His father was a minister. Reverend Rubicon made the circuit of the state's Freewill Baptist churches. Some of Rubicon's earliest memories were of sitting in hardwood pews and fidgeting and squirming, wishing his father would get done with the sermon so they could leave. His father was also prominent in the American Anti-Slavery Society and high in the ranks of the Temperance Society. It kept him so busy that Rubicon rarely got to see him. Which was fine by Rubicon.

They had lived in a small frame house on the outskirts of Coopersville, with miles and miles of woodland out their back door. As a boy Rubicon spent every spare moment he could in those woods. He learned the ways of the animals. He learned to hunt and fish. His father didn't approve, but the good reverend prided himself on being fair-minded and on letting the young grow as they saw fit, with the result that shortly after he turned sixteen Rubicon packed his few belongings, bid his father and those church pews good-bye, and headed west.

Rubicon had heard a lot about the frontier, about mountains that reared to the clouds and prairies as vast as the sea and deep woods where no man had ever set foot. All that turned out to be true. Unfortunately, though, while he was adept at living off the land, he still needed money. He refused to make his own clothes when he could buy them. Then there were things like guns and ammunition and coffee and blankets.

A few scrapes with hostiles gave Rubicon the opinion that the whites were right and the only good red man was a dead red man. So when fate drew him and Venom to the same card table at a cantina in Taos, their small talk led to Rubicon becoming a scalp hunter.

If his reverend pa could see him now, Rubicon reflected, it would put him in his grave. Provided his father wasn't already six feet under. It had been a dozen years since Rubicon struck off on his own, and for all he knew both his parents were dead. He wouldn't lose any sleep if they were. They never had seen eye to eye on much.

Take that slavery business. The reverend had thundered every Sunday from the pulpit about how downtrodden the blacks in the South were and how vile slavery was and how the abominable institution should be abolished. He wanted Rubicon to join the Anti-Slavery Society, but Rubicon refused.

"Have you no conscience, boy?" his father once asked. "Your skin is the same color as theirs. They're your brothers and your sisters. We must do what we can to ease their plight."

Rubicon had laughed. "Ma only ever gave birth

to me. I don't have any brothers or sisters. As for my skin, a bay horse is the same color as a black bear. That's doesn't mean the horse should let the bear eat it."

"You make no sense."

It did to Rubicon. He saw his color as an accident of birth. He could just as well have been born white or red or yellow. So what if other blacks were used as slaves. *He* wasn't, and the only one in his world that mattered was him.

Rubicon remembered how upset his father had been, and grinned. The reverend and his high-and-mighty ways. Always claiming to be right about everything because he lived by the Bible.

That was another thing Rubicon could go the rest of his days without. He had been sick to death of his father always quoting from Scripture. If he had heard "thou shall not" one more time, he would have screamed.

Once more Rubicon grinned, but it promptly faded. He had found where his quarry stopped to rest. Dismounting, he squatted beside a hoofprint and pinched some of the dirt between his thumb and index finger. He reckoned he was an hour behind, maybe a little less.

Hefting his rifle, Rubicon climbed on his horse and used his heels. Venom's orders were to track them but not show himself. He must wait for the others to catch up. Venom claimed it was for his own safety, but Rubicon wasn't fooled. Venom wanted to be in on the catch and the kill.

The tracks continued to the west. Rubicon figured they were making for the foothills. The timbered slopes might seem to offer them sanctuary, but they were fools if they thought they could shake him.

When he was on a trail he was like a hound on a scent. He never gave up. He'd follow them to the ends of the earth, if that was what it took to bring them to bay.

Rubicon rose in the stirrups and scanned the horizon. There was no sign of them. He must be careful not to get too close until after the sun went down or they might spot him.

His rifle across his saddle, Rubicon rode at a leisurely pace. He came to a gully and went down it and up the other side. Beyond were more, an erosion-worn maze that would slow the white girl and her friends. Their tracks led down into another and along the bottom.

Rubicon wondered about those friends of hers. He'd never run across Indians who dyed their buckskins green. Mostly, Indians wore ordinary buckskins, or breechclouts like the Apaches sometimes did.

The tracks led around a bend.

Rubicon was almost to it when his horse pricked its ears. Instantly, he drew rein. He listened, but all he heard was the long grass whispering in the breeze.

Alighting, Rubicon let the reins dangle and catfooted to the bend. A familiar tingle rippled down his spine, a sensation he felt when danger was about to break over him like a wave over a beach. He checked the right rim and the left rim.

A bee buzzed about a flower.

Rubicon crouched, every sense straining. He noted that his shadow was behind him and wouldn't give him away when he crept forward. As silently as a stalking cat, he edged around the bend. No one was there. Rubicon started to lower his rifle.

"Stand as still as can be," said the white girl's voice, "or so help me God I'll blow out your wick."

Venom's anger grew to where he abruptly drew rein and wheeled his mount. His company halted, their expressions adding to his anger. "Well?" he demanded.

"Well what?" Potter responded.

"Let's hear it."

"Hear what?" This from Tibbet.

"Not one of you has said a word for miles. Out with it. Let me hear who thinks I did wrong."

They looked at one another and one of the Kyler twins, it had to be Jeph by the nick in his ear, scratched his chin and said, "Not me or my brother. You put up with more from him than we would."

Seph nodded. "It served him right for doin' to girls what he done. I'll kill 'em and I'll take their hair, but it's not right to do the other."

"It's sick," Jeph said.

"How about the rest of you?" Venom prompted, knowing full well none of the others had the grit to stand up to him.

Potter pursed his thick lips. "I'm not saying it was wrong. I'm not saying Logan shouldn't have sassed you like he done. I am saying we should have buried him."

"Since when did you turn Christian?"

"Now, now. You asked us. I've never liked to leave anyone aboveground when they should be below it."

"You'll scalp a ten-year-old Comanche boy, but you're squeamish about leaving bodies for the coyotes to eat?" Venom had always considered Potter an idiot, and this did nothing to raise his estimation. "I swear, some of you don't have the sense God gave a goat."

"We do the best we can," Potter assured him.

Venom reminded himself that for all their faults, they had stayed loyal to him through all sorts of hardships. "Look. It wasn't just his sass that got Logan dead. It was how he acted all the time, always prodding me, always giving the notion he could do a better job at leading this outfit. I put up with it longer than I should have because he always held his own in a fight and that's when we need each other the most. But there are limits to what a man will take and he pushed me over mine."

"No need to explain, boss," said Calvert.

"Yes, there is. We can't have hard feelings. We have to always cover the other's back. It's why I don't let just anyone join us. I only pick those I think we can depend on. I only pick the best." Venom was flattering them to win them over. He had learned long ago that a carrot worked a lot better than a stick at keeping them content.

"Shucks, boss," Tibbet said proudly. "We have full pokes thanks to you. There's not one of us who won't cover your back when you need it covered."

Venom smiled. "That's what I like to hear." He headed west again. It wasn't long before he came on one of Rubicon's marks. It made him think of the time he'd asked the black how he got such a strange name. Rubicon said it had been his pa's idea, that his pa always intended to stay single, but when he met Rubicon's mom, he'd given in to temptation and crossed the Rubicon, whatever the hell that was.

A killdeer's shrill cry brought Venom out of himself. The bird was pretending it had a broken wing and running in circles to get them to go after it and lead them away from its mate and their nest. Venom almost shot it out of spite.

The warm sun and the steady rhythm of his horse

began to make Venom drowsy. He stifled a yawn and shook himself. A buffalo wallow appeared, and then another, and yet a third. Since most of the buffs had migrated, he didn't give any thought to them until a loud grunt heralded the rise of a massive form from out of a wallow partially hidden by high grass.

"Hell," Venom said, and reined up.

The bull glared and pawed the earth. It was an old bull, well past its prime, its left horn broken.

"Shoot it!" Potter whispered.

Bulls often gathered in small herds when they weren't battling for harems. The really old ones became loners and wandered the prairie until disease or wolves or something else brought them down.

"What are you waiting for?"

"Hush, you yack," Venom whispered back. He'd rather let the bull go its ornery way if the bull would let them do the same.

The buff snorted and stamped and shook its huge head.

Venom hoped it wouldn't charge. He couldn't afford to lose any of his men. Worse, he might lose a horse. "Stay still, everyone," he commanded. "We don't want to rile this critter."

The bull took a few lumbering steps while rumbling deep in its barrel chest. Again it tossed its head and gouged the ground with a heavy front hoof.

"Damn it," Venom said under his breath. He thumbed back the hammer on his rifle and curled his finger around the trigger. It was a .75-caliber Brown Bess he had taken from a Mexican he shot and scalped, and could drop just about any animal this side of a whale. But he'd rather not put it to the test against the buff's inches-thick skull.

The bull kept stomping and snorting.

Venom took a gamble. The buff was working it-self up to attack. Maybe it would calm down if they showed that they meant it no harm. Accordingly, he reined to the left to go around.

The buffalo's beady eyes followed him.

"Stay where you are, you mangy son of a bitch," Venom said, holding his mount to a walk. Over his shoulder he cautioned his men, "Nice and easy does it, boys."

"We should ride like hell," Tibbet suggested.

Suddenly the bull turned and lumbered back down into the wallow and out of sight.

Potter uttered a nervous laugh. "Thank goodness! I thought for sure it would charge."

Tibbet laughed, too. "We were lucky. The only thing worse than an angry griz is an angry buff."

Venom twisted to tell them to shut the hell up, that they weren't out of danger yet and should keep quiet until the wallow was well behind them. He was a shade too late.

Up and over the bank hurtled the old bull. It came at them so fast that it was on them before practi-cally any of them could get off a shot. The twins did. Jeph and Seph fired at the same split second. The bull stumbled, but it didn't go down. It only slowed and then it was up and at full speed again, its head lowered to ram and gore.

Venom took aim but didn't shoot. The bull wasn't broadside, and he wanted it broadside in order to be sure to hit its vitals.

Most of the others were trying to rein to safety.

Potter had his horse halfway around when the bull rammed into it with an audible crunch. His scream and the screech of his stricken mount pre-ceded the crash of both to the hard earth.

"Help me!" Raw fear twisted Potter's face as he frantically sought to push clear. Above him, the bull dug at his mount's belly with its good horn. The horse whinnied and kicked and struggled to rise, but the bull had it pinned to the earth. Intestines oozed from a widening cavity.

Venom gigged his own animal, not away from the bull as some of the others were doing but toward it. He pressed the Brown Bess to his shoulder and the moment he had the target he wanted, he fired. The Brown Bess thundered and spat smoke and lead. He'd hoped to drop the bull in its tracks, but it wasn't to be. No sooner did he fire than the brute left off goring Potter's horse and wheeled with astounding swiftness for a creature so immense.

"Look out!" Tibbet hollered.

"It's charging again!" Ryson yelled.

Venom didn't need the warning. He could see that the bull had a new victim picked out.

It was him.

Chapter Twelve

Logan opened his eyes and was racked with pain. He thought it strange since by rights he should be dead. He remembered Venom pointing a pistol at him. He'd tried to twist aside, but his reflexes were no match for a bullet. He remembered the blast of the shot, remembered the shock of being hit. Then he was falling and the ground rushed up to meet him and after that there was nothing but darkness until now.

Sliding his hands under him, Logan rose onto his elbows. His head pounded, and his stomach churned. Gingerly, he touched his temple and winced. From near his eyebrow to above his ear was a lead-gouged furrow. Probably because he was turning when Venom fired, the bullet had struck a glancing blow. It was the only reason he was alive. Judging by the circle of red under him and the amount of dry blood on his face and neck, he'd bled a lot.

Logan sat up. He wasn't surprised to find that his rifle and pistols and knife were gone. His former friends had helped themselves to his weapons. To his horse, too.

With great care, Logan slowly stood. Dizziness struck and he swayed but stayed on his feet. Lightly pressing his hand to the wound, he walked in a small circle, establishing that the tracks of his former companions, as he figured they would, pointed to the west. He plodded after them.

With each passing minute the pain subsided a little so that by the end of half an hour it was a persistent dull ache. His queasiness faded, too. Logan thought of Venom and clenched his fists. The bastard had shot him without warning and left him for dead. No one did that to him and went on breathing. No one.

In a way, Venom had done him a favor. For some time now Logan had considered either taking over the company or going off and starting one of his own. He was tired of the looks he got from the others when he indulged in females, tired of them always carping about what he did. They had no room to talk, the hypocrites. They carved up women and girls to add to their scalp bag. All he did differently was enjoy the ladies before he scalped them.

Logan got hooked when he was young. An aunt started him down the path. She'd liked it rough, really rough, and given him a taste that grew rougher as time went by. Now when he was done with a woman, she looked as if she'd been through a war. Most were barely alive.

He couldn't get enough. It gave him a thrill like no other. A thrill so potent, he couldn't go without. When he wasn't with a woman, he daydreamed about being with them, and at night he drifted in dreams of explicit fantasy.

Unfortunately, the law hanged people for what he did.

So Logan had gone off to the frontier where tin badges were scarce and he could do pretty much as he pleased. The frontier, where Indians were usually blamed for whites who went missing and whites were blamed for Indians who went missing.

At first it had been heaven on earth. He'd waylaid women and had his way and no one was ever the wiser. But his habit didn't put food in his belly or clothes on his back. He needed spending money.

Logan happened to be in San Antonio one hot afternoon when Venom and his scalp hunters rode in to claim the bounty on some Comanche scalps. Logan approached Venom about working for him and was pleased as could be when the veteran took him on. His pleasure was short-lived. The third time out, they slaughtered a family of peaceable Pimas. Logan got hold of a girl about fourteen and before he could stop himself had done the sort of things that always sent a tingle of delight down his spine.

That had led to this, to being betrayed and shot down like some animal. The more Logan thought about it, the madder he got. He would keep going until he got hold of a horse and then he would find Venom and his so-called friends and do to them as they had done to him.

Along the way Logan intended to treat himself. He needed a female, needed a female bad. Specifically, the white girl Rubicon told them about. The young one, the pretty one. He would do to her as he had done to all those others.

Logan couldn't wait.

Evelyn warned the black man not to move or she would shoot him. She assumed the threat would turn him to stone. Instead, as she rose from concealment on the crest of the gully with her Hawken centered on his chest, he did the last thing she expected.

The black turned and smiled, his arms out from

his sides. "We meet again, young one," he cheerfully greeted her.

"Didn't you hear me?" Evelyn demanded. "I'll shoot you if you don't do exactly as I say."

"Shot a lot of people, have you? Somehow, I don't think so. I doubt you've ever shot anybody." He confidently added, "It's never easy the first time. Some people can't do it. They don't have it in them."

"I do," Evelyn assured him. With a bob of her chin at the opposite side of the gully, she said, "So does he."

Plenty Elk had an arrow nocked to his bowstring and the string drawn back to his cheek.

"Don't do anything hasty," the black man said. "See? I'm putting my rifle down. Now I'm taking a pistol and laying it down, too."

"I told you not to move, scalp hunter." Evelyn held the Hawken straight and steady, ready to shoot. He was right, though. She wasn't like her brother. She wasn't a killer. She wouldn't shoot unless he forced her, and even then she would shoot reluctantly.

The black raised his hands in the air. "Suit yourself, girl. You caught me fair and square. But what was that about scalps?"

"Play innocent, why don't you?"

"Why, girl, I'm as innocent as a newborn babe."

Evelyn sidled down the slope. She told him to get on his knees. He hesitated, glanced at Plenty Elk, and did as she bid him. With Plenty Elk covering her, Evelyn reached around from behind and snatched the second pistol, then stepped back. "There now. We need to talk. First off, what's your name?"

"Rubicon."

"That's a strange name. What does it mean?"

Rubicon shrugged. "My pa said it had something to do with a river somewhere. That's all I know."

"Plenty Elk, here, has told me about you and your friends. How far back are they? What are their plans? Were you to signal them when you caught up with us?"

"You ask a lot of questions," Rubicon said good-naturedly.

"I expect a lot of answers." It had been Evelyn's idea to take him alive. Plenty Elk had been disappointed, but she convinced him the black might have information they could use.

Rubicon chuckled. "Listen to yourself. You're a girl playing at being tough. If you had any sense you would get on your horse and ride like hell while you still can."

"Big talk, but *we* caught *you*, not the other way around."

"It's not me you have to worry about, girl. It's the man I ride for. He'll be awful mad at you for jumping me and he's not nice when he's mad. Fact is, he's the meanest cuss on the whole damn planet."

"I'm a King, mister."

"Is that supposed to mean something?"

"It means I might be a girl, but I'm not helpless. It means I never give up. It means I don't desert my friends. It means I'll do whatever I have to in order to stop you."

"For a fool you sure are pretty."

"On your feet. Keep your hands where I can see them and head up this gully." Evelyn snagged the reins to his horse and brought it along.

Rubicon chuckled. "Get on my knees. Get on my feet. I wish you'd make up your mind."

"You're in awful good spirits for someone in your predicament."

"It's not me who has the predicament, girl. It's you. I don't know what you think you're doing by

taking me this way. It won't do you any good. It
won't do you any good at all."

"Why do you ride with the man you told me
about? You don't strike me as being bad."

Rubicon glanced over his shoulder at her. "There
you go again. Missy, you can't judge other folks by
how you think. It's how *they* think that counts. You
better let me go or the first chance I get, I'll beat you
to the ground and I won't bat an eye doing it."

"Get moving." Evelyn saw Plenty Elk give her a
quizzical look. She motioned for him to come down
and he was quick to fall into step beside her. Not
once did he lower his bow.

"Yes, sir," Rubicon rambled on. "You're in a fine
pickle. You won't take my advice and light a shuck.
What to do? What to do?"

"You like to hear yourself talk, don't you?"

Rubicon was talking to distract her, and to test
how much she would let him get away with. He was
trying to dupe her into letting down her guard so he
could jump her. Otherwise, he was in for grief when
Venom caught up. Venom didn't like it when his
men were taken captive. The last man that happened
to, a gent by the name of Williams, was staked out
in the burning sun by the Comanches. Venom refused to cut him free, saying that anyone so damn
careless had it coming to them.

Evelyn was glad her captive had gone quiet. All
his chatter was making it hard for her to think, and
she had a lot to work out. She could tell that Plenty
Elk was puzzled that she hadn't killed the man out-
right, and to be honest, the smart thing was to shoot
him dead. She'd had the perfect opportunity back
there and couldn't do it. It worried her. By civilized
standards she'd done the right thing. Only this
wasn't civilization. This was the wilderness. The

laws and rules that people stuck to east of the Mississippi River did not apply west of it. Out here it was be strong and live or be weak and die.

For a long while now, Evelyn had secretly wondered if she was weak. There were incidents in the past, times when she should have slain someone out to do her harm, and she didn't. She couldn't find it in her. Maybe—and the thought troubled her—maybe she was one of those who couldn't harm another living soul no matter what the circumstances.

Her father killed when he had to. Her brother did it time and time again with no remorse. Even her mother had taken a life or two. What was wrong with her that she couldn't do the same?

Evelyn put it from her mind. Now wasn't the time. They rounded the next bend and there were the Nansusequa, anxiously waiting. "Look what we found," she announced.

"Why is he not dead?" Waku asked.

"We're taking him with us. First I need someone to tie his wrists. Dega, would you do the honors? There's a rope in my parfleche."

Dega was happy to do anything she asked. The mare shied when he reached for the saddle, but Evelyn spoke to it and the horse stood still while he opened the parfleche and took out the rope Evelyn used to tether the mare at night. Drawing his knife, he cut a suitable length and replaced the rest. As he walked over behind the captive, the black man grinned.

"Tell me, green boy, do you savvy the white tongue?"

"I speak white," Dega said. "And I not be green."

"Your buckskins are." Rubicon bobbed his chin at the rest of the family. "So are theirs. What gives?"

"No give you our clothes. Our clothes ours."

Rubicon blinked, and chortled. "No, no. What I want to know is why are you dressed all in green?"

"Green for Manitoa," Dega explained. "Green for life."

"Not green for grass?" Rubicon taunted.

"Put hands back so I tie them."

"Sure, whatever you say." Rubicon moved his arms behind him and felt his wrists gripped.

"Not move," Dega directed.

"You'll get to go on breathing if you cooperate," Evelyn said.

"I'm all for breathing."

Dega gave the rope a shake. "Once you tied we no danger."

"That's what you think." Rubicon noticed that the girl had lowered her rifle partway. The Arapaho still had an arrow notched to his bow, but the boy about to tie his wrists had stepped between them. No one else had a weapon ready to use. They were green in more ways than one, these people, and it was about to cost them. Suddenly stiffening, he looked back the way they had come and yelled, "Venom! Potter! It's about time you got here."

The ruse worked. All of them turned. Every last one. Even the boy with the rope.

Rubicon whirled. He had the boy's tomahawk in his hand before any of them could think to stop him. He swung it and caught the boy across the head with the flat of the blade. He'd meant to cleave the boy's head, but in his haste he misjudged his swing.

Plenty Elk saw Degamawaku start to fall. He stepped to the right for a clear target and took a split second to sight down the arrow. At that range he could hardly miss, but he was going for the heart, for a kill shot, and he wanted to be sure.

Rubicon expected the Arapaho to react first. The Dog Eater was seven or eight feet away, too far to hit. So Rubicon threw the tomahawk. He didn't expect to inflict a wound, only to make the Arapaho duck and buy him the time to grab a gun from the girl.

The tomahawk spun end over end.

Plenty Elk went to fling himself aside and was turning when the tomahawk struck his bow and glanced off. The keen edge caught him in the side of the neck, slicing through skin, flesh and blood vessels. He clutched at himself as a red mist sprayed every which way.

"Plenty Elk!" Evelyn cried. She jerked her rifle up. With a howl of triumph, Rubicon was on her.

Chapter Thirteen

Venom had no time to rein around, no time to spur his horse. He felt no fear, no panic. Bracing for the impact, he hiked his leg clear of the stirrup.

In a flurry of driving hooves, the bull crossed the space separating them. Just as it lowered its head to rip and gore, its front legs buckled and it crashed heavily to the ground, its momentum carrying it past Venom and his mount, missing them by a hand's width.

A twitch of the bull's tail, a final grunt, and it was dead.

"That was close!" Potter exclaimed. He had managed to push out from under his horse and was rubbing his left leg.

"You must have nerves of steel," Tibbet threw in. "Sitting there as calm as could be."

"I'm proud to ride with a man like you," Jeph Kyler said, and his twin nodded in agreement.

Venom hadn't done it to impress them. Still, anything that made them fear him more made it that much less likely they would cause him trouble. "We're losing time," he said, and reined around.

"Wait!" Potter hollered. "What about me?"

"Throw your saddle on one of the Injun ponies

we took and be quick about it." Venom chafed at the delay. He was eager to catch up to Rubicon and see the white girl. From the way Rubicon had described her, she must be about the prettiest young filly this side of the cradle.

The Kyler twins came up on either side.

"Want us to go on ahead and see how the darkie is doin'?" Jeph asked.

"Rubicon knows how to take care of himself."

"That he does," Seph agreed. "But there are seven of them and one is an Arapaho warrior."

Venom still didn't see the need, but since he preferred to stay on the twins' good side, he replied, "I'd rather you stay with us, but go on if you want." To his annoyance, they did. That left him with four, this close to Sioux territory. "Hurry up with that damn saddle, Potter."

For the next several hours they rode nearly due west. Around them the prairie was awash in the golden glow of the sun. Butterflies flitted amid patches of wildflowers. Jackrabbits bounded off in incredibly long leaps. A red fox watched them go by, unafraid.

Venom supposed there were those who would call the prairie beautiful or God's handiwork or some such. He wasn't one of them. Grass was grass, flowers were flowers. As for the Almighty, he stopped believing the day he saw a little boy's head crushed by the flailing hoof of a horse.

Toward the middle of the afternoon Venom was surprised to see the twins galloping back. He raised his arm and the others stopped to await them. "Don't keep me in suspense," he said as the pair reined to a stop.

"Indians," Seph declared. "Thirty or forty. Northwest of here, heading east."

"They'll pass within a quarter mile of you," Jeph took up the account. "We felt you should know."

"Could you tell which tribe?"

"They were too far off. If I had to guess, I'd say Sioux, but that's a hunch more than anything."

Venom reined to the south. "We'll go a mile or so out of our way so they don't spot us."

They went less than a quarter of that when Venom drew abrupt rein. To the southwest was a dust cloud. Only two things raised that much dust; a lot of buffalo or a lot of riders. He got out his spyglass. "Indians," he announced. An awful lot of Indians.

"It can't be the same bunch we saw," one of the twins said.

"They're heading northeast and will miss us by a good long way," Venom calculated.

Potter anxiously remarked, "This country is crawling with the red heathens."

"Maybe they're looking for us," Tibbet speculated.

"Or that girl and her friends," Calvert said.

"Or that freight train," Ryson threw in.

Venom had a different notion. "I bet they're holding a powwow. Maybe they're fixing to go on the war path against the Shoshones or some other enemy and the bands are gathering. Just our luck we happen to be passing through."

Potter was glancing every which way. "We'll have to be extra careful from here on out."

Venom blistered the air with oaths. This would slow them. At the rate things were going, they wouldn't catch up to Rubicon until sometime tomorrow.

"Yes, sir," Potter said. "We'll be turned into pincushions if we don't keep our eyes peeled."

Venom swore some more. He needed this like he

needed a bullet hole in the head. "We'll wait until this bunch is out of sight before we move on." He leaned on his saddle horn.

"It's too bad you had to shoot Logan," Potter said. "We could use his gun if it comes to a fight."

"Good riddance," Venom growled.

The sun was about to set.

Logan had hiked for miles and his Texas boots weren't fashioned for a lot of walking. His feat ached something awful. His head still ached, too. He would dearly love a chug of whiskey, but his flask had been in his saddlebags.

Logan thought of the white girl and what he would do to her. It had been too long since the last one. To make up for it he would take his time with her and draw it out as long as he could.

Logan was so lost in his daydream that he almost missed spotting an orange glow to the northwest. "A campfire," he blurted, and stopped. He doubted it was Venom and the company. They were well to the west by now. Nor could it be the freighters. Their wagons were canvas-topped turtles and couldn't have come this far. That left an army patrol, another party of whites—or Indians.

Logan debated. He looked down at his sore feet. He gnawed his lower lip. Finally he bent his steps toward the glow. He hoped he wasn't making a mistake. But where there were men there were horses and he could dearly use a horse.

The glow turned out to be farther away than it appeared. Full dark had fallen when Logan came close enough to distinguish figures and to hear voices that warned him it wasn't a patrol or other whites.

Dropping onto his belly, Logan crawled.

The fire was small, typical of Indians. The dozen

or so warriors hunkered around it had paint on their faces. Some of the horses had paint on them, too. Bows and lances were the favored weapons. Only one had a rifle, which looked to be an old Hudson's Bay trade gun.

Logan lay in the dark and bided his time.

The warriors talked in low tones. They had brought down a buck earlier and were roasting a haunch.

The tantalizing aroma set Logan's mouth to watering. Crossing his arms in front of him, he rested his chin on his wrist. He made slits of his eyes so the fire shine didn't give him away. Now all he could do was wait.

Usually Indians turned in early. Early compared to whites, anyhow. Logan listened to the drone of their voices and felt his blood grow sluggish in his veins. He started to drift off but snapped his eyes open and shook himself. Too late he saw a warrior coming toward him, maybe to heed nature's call. Whatever the reason, the warrior spotted him at the same instant and let out a yip of alarm.

Pushing upright, Logan spun and raced off. The warrior ran after him. Others leaped to their feet and swarmed in pursuit.

Logan ran with all his speed, but he had never been especially fleet of foot. He heard the smack of the warrior's moccasins close on his heels. They were flying through the dark, no more than inky silhouettes. It was nearly impossible to see much, and that gave Logan an idea. Abruptly stopping, he sidestepped and unleashed an uppercut. It caught the onrushing warrior full on the jaw and flattened him like a flapjack.

Pain exploded up Logan's arm, but he ignored it and groped at the warrior's waist. Nearly every warrior carried a knife. A smooth hilt molded to his palm, and drawing the blade, he slashed the warrior's throat. Then he turned and ran.

The other warriors weren't far behind. They had lost sight of him and spread out.

Logan heard horses coming. He glanced back and counted three riders. They were spreading out, too.

Howls of outrage told him they had found their slain friend.

Logan ran another dozen feet and threw himself flat. Twisting around, he held the bloody knife close to his cheek. A warrior ran past on his left. Another pounded by on the right. The grass was high enough that neither spotted him.

Finally, Logan had what he'd been waiting for; a mounted Sioux approached. The warrior yelled something. A warrior on foot answered and the mounted Sioux reined toward him. The horse passed within a few feet of where Logan lay. Coiling his legs, Logan tensed.

The warrior was searching right and left, looking everywhere except down.

Logan catapulted upward, his arm stiff and straight. The blade sank deep into the warrior's belly. Warm blood gushed over Logan's hand as the Sioux grunted and stiffened and opened his mouth to cry out.

Logan wrenched on the blade, hard. Out spilled intestines and whatever else a man had inside him. Logan grabbed a wrist and yanked. Thankfully, the horse didn't spook. Another moment, and he was on it and galloping away, doubled over so the warriors he passed wouldn't realize he was white.

It almost worked. Logan was about to be swallowed by the night when whoops and a commotion warned him he had been spotted.

He got out of there.

Arrows whizzed past. A lance arced out of the stars and thudded into the earth.

What Logan wouldn't give for a gun! He had a horse, though, and a knife, and once he shook the Sioux, he could get on with tracking Venom and the girl and her friends and treat himself to hours of pure pleasure.

He tingled at the prospect.

Evelyn swung her rifle toward Rubicon, but he grabbed the barrel and swung the Hawken and her both, with no more effort than she would swing a stick. She tripped and stumbled and almost fell. Digging in her heels, she sought to wrest the rifle free, but he was much too strong. She was vaguely aware of some of the others yelling, and of Plenty Elk on the ground, spraying scarlet.

Rubicon backhanded her. He had dropped the boy in green and the Dog Eater, but there was still the father, somewhere behind him. He needed the rifle and he needed it now. With a powerful shove, he sent the girl sprawling. Grinning, he spun, thinking he had them beat. He was halfway around when a sharp pang jarred him and a prickly sensation shot through his innards. He glanced down at the knife hilt jutting from his body and then at the man who had killed him. "Son of a bitch," he blurted as a veil of ink fell.

Waku pulled his blade free and stepped back. His wife and daughters were safe to one side, Tihi with her arms protectively around the girls. He stepped to his son, who was attempting to stand. "Lie still."

"Evelyn . . ." Dega said, blood trickling from a gash in his temple.

"I'm here." Evelyn was bruised but otherwise unhurt. She snatched up her Hawken and knelt next to Waku. "How is he?"

Probing gingerly, Waku said in relief, "He is not hurt bad. He will live."

Forgetting herself, Evelyn clasped Dega's hand. "Thank God. My heart about stopped when I saw him hit you."

Dega's own heart beat faster. She rarely touched him. The warm feel of her fingers was like a tonic. New vigor pumped through him, and he smiled in delight. "I happy you like me."

"Why wouldn't I?" Evelyn said. "We're friends, aren't we?" She immediately turned to Plenty Elk, who was on his back, deathly still and deathly pale. His buckskins and the grass around him were drenched. The wound was hideous, inches deep and jagged. She touched his cheek and his eyes opened.

Plenty Elk weakly raised his hands. 'I die now.'

'I much sad,' Evelyn signed. She had only known him a short while, but she had liked him a lot. She yearned to help, but there was nothing she could do. He had lost too much blood.

'You good friend.'

'Thank you help us,' Evelyn responded, and winced inside. He was dying because he had stuck with them instead of striking off for his village and his people. 'You good friend same.'

Plenty Elk tried to sign more, but his arms fell to his sides and he twitched a few times. His eyes sought hers.

Evelyn held his hand and swallowed a lump in her throat. She did not know what else to do, what else to sign. She rubbed his hand and smiled.

Plenty Elk smiled back. A tender look came over him. Then a soft gasp escaped him. His eyes shifted to the sky and widened, and with his next exhale, life fled.

"I'm so sorry." Evelyn gently closed his glazing

eyes. She turned back to Dega. He had sat up and was holding his head in his hands. Placing her hand on his shoulder, she said softly, "I still have you."

Dega wanted the pounding between his ears to stop so he could think again. "Always have me," he assured her.

Waku looked at them and at his wife. Rising, he took a few steps to the east, blood dripping from his knife onto his moccasins. "We must ride fast, Evelyn King."

Evelyn knew what he was thinking. The rest of the scalp hunters were still after them. Sooner or later they would catch up, and more people were bound to die.

A lot more.

Chapter Fourteen

"Who do you think is buried in the graves?" Tibbet wondered.

"How the hell do I know?" Venom snapped. "I can't see through dirt." He had a hunch, though, about one of them. "Dig them up."

"Dig up dead bodies?" Potter said apprehensively.

"They wouldn't be buried if they were alive." Some days Venom had no patience with Potter's stupidity and this was one of them.

"That's not what I meant. They've been dead hours. They'll smell and have started to swell."

"So hold your nose." Venom turned away before he shot him. He was in a foul temper. Thanks to the delays, the girl and her green-clad friends were now hours ahead. He went over to the Kyler twins, who were standing by their mounts.

"You two are the best trackers I've got after Rubicon. I want you to go on ahead. Track the girl and her party, but don't let them see you. Leave marks for us. We'll come along as fast as we can."

Jeph nodded at the mounds of earth. "You reckon one of them is the black, don't you?"

"Unless he killed a couple and went on after the rest, but he'd never have bothered to bury them."

"The girl and her green Indians must have jumped him," Seph said.

Venom scowled. "Rubicon always did what I told him, and I told him not to tangle with them. If he's in one of those graves, then yes, somehow they caught on that he was tracking them and killed him."

"They ain't harmless then," Jeph said.

"Whoever said they were?" Venom gestured. "On your way. Keep your eyes skinned. I don't care to lose you two, too."

"Don't worry about us. The black only had two eyes and two ears. We have four."

"Too much confidence can get you killed," Venom cautioned.

"Better too much than too little," was Seph's rebuttal.

They climbed on and rode off. Venom watched until they were out of sight, then stepped to where Potter, Tibbet, Calvert and Ryson were scooping the fresh dirt away with their hands. Potter's face was twisted in disgust.

"It's only dirt, you idiot," Ryson chided.

Potter wiped a sleeve across his sweat-speckled brow. "It's what's under the dirt. The dead spook me."

"Why? What can they do to you?"

"It's how they look. Pasty and bloated and all. I can't stand to touch them. It gives me shivers."

"If it wasn't that you can shoot and cook, you'd be worthless," Calvert put in.

Potter stopped scooping. "Here now. Why are you mad at me? What did I do?"

"You're breathing." Venom stabbed a finger at the mound. "Dig, damn you. I don't intend to stand around here all day." He scoured the plain, then sat down a few yards away with his rifle across his legs.

"Strange, isn't it?" Tibbet said while scooping.

"What?"

"The girl took the time to bury them. She must know we're after them, but she did it anyway."

Venom leaned back. The sun was low in the west. They only had an hour or so of daylight left. "That's the difference between people like her and people like us. It tells you a lot about her."

"How so?"

"We wouldn't have bothered. We'd have left these two to rot, even if one is Rubicon, and pushed on." Venom paused. "This girl couldn't bring herself to ride off and leave them lying there. That shows she's got a good heart. She went to the trouble to plant them, knowing every minute she delayed was a minute closer we came. That shows she's got grit."

"A good heart and grit won't stop her from being dead," Ryson said.

"No one is to harm her unless I say," Venom warned. "I might have another use for her before we kill her."

Several of them laughed.

Potter mopped his brow again. "Say, how do we know she's not in one of these graves?"

Venom gave a start. He hadn't thought of that.

"Here!" Tibbet bawled. "I found a hand!"

"Get excited, why don't you?" Venom said. "It's the body the hand's attached to that I want to see."

They dug with renewed vigor and in no time exposed a young Arapaho warrior, his hands folded across his chest, his face so pale he was whiter than a white.

"Cut in the neck," Tibbet observed aloud.

Venom stood and went to the body. "The last of the four we jumped. We don't have to worry about word getting back to the Araphaos. Uncover the other one."

It took barely a minute. Rubicon's features were waxen, his mouth curled in a grimace. His arms, too, had been folded across his chest, and his eyes were closed.

"He looks like he's sleeping," Potter said.

"He is. Forever," Calvert remarked.

Tibbet squatted and indicated a red stain on Rubicon's shirt. "He was stabbed. They jumped him, I bet. He'd never let them get close enough, otherwise."

Venom turned to his mount. "Let's go. We still have daylight left."

"Don't you want us to bury them again?" Potter asked.

"I'm not the girl. I don't have a good heart. Let the coyotes and the buzzards fatten their bellies." Venom's saddle creaked as he forked leather and hooked his feet in the stirrups.

"Even Rubicon?"

Venom sighed. "Haven't you gotten it through your head yet? You're only of use to me while you're breathing. Once you stop, I don't give a damn what happens. Now get on your damn horse and quit asking damn stupid questions." He took the lead. They wouldn't be able to go far before darkness claimed the prairie, but that was all right. Morning would come soon enough.

"Tomorrow you're mine, girl," Venom vowed.

Evelyn rode until well after the sun went down. She would have pushed on until midnight, but little Mikikawaku could barely sit her saddle and the rest of the family showed signs of severe fatigue. Reluctantly, Evelyn stopped in the middle of a basin and announced, "We'll spend the night here."

Dega touched the gash in his temple. "It good we stop. I not feel well."

Evelyn was worried he had a concussion. She swung down to help him dismount.

"I do it my own self." Dega refused to be weak in front of her. He slowly alighted, then had to lean against his horse when dizziness threatened to buckle his legs.

"Are you all right?"

"I fine," Dega lied.

Tihikanima put her arm around her son's shoulders. "Sit," she directed. "Let me look at your head."

"I just told Evelyn I am fine, Mother."

"You try too hard to impress her." Tihi examined the wound and touched a dry drop of blood. "You were fortunate he struck you with the flat side of the tomahawk."

Dega sank onto his back and placed his forearm across his forehead. "I want sleep."

Evelyn opened her parfleche. Inside was a bundle of pemmican and another that contained herbs her mother used to heal and cure. The Shoshones had treatments for all sorts of ailments and injuries. Everything from grinding sagebrush leaves into powder to use on the rash on a baby's bottom to balsam root to ward off ticks to the fuzz from prickly pear cactus for removing warts.

At the moment Evelyn was looking for what the Shoshones called *unda vich quana*. They used it on wounds. She crushed a dry leaf in her palm, then went over and knelt next to Dega. "I have something here that will help you."

"I drink or eat?"

"Neither. I have to rub it on. It'll hurt some, but in a while the pain will go away."

"What did she say?" Tihi asked.

Dega translated.

"Tell her I will take care of you. I have medicine in my pack." Tihi went to rise but Dega gripped her wrist.

"I thank you, but I would like her to treat me."

"You choose her over your mother?"

Dega didn't say anything.

"I have nursed you since you were an infant. Every scrape, every bruise, the time you burned your fingers in the fire, the time you broke a finger when you fell from a tree, the time you sprained your ankle and it was so swollen you could hardly walk on it, and many more."

"No son ever had a better mother."

"Then why her over me?"

Evelyn had listened to the exchange in growing puzzlement. "Is something the matter?"

"All be fine," Dega assured her.

"Why does Tihi look upset?"

"She not like me hurt." To his mother Dega said, "It is not her over you. No one can ever take your place."

"Yet you want her to dress your wound." Tihi unfurled and sadly remarked, "Every mother knows this day will come. It is not a day we look forward to."

"What are you talking about?"

"The day when another is as important as a mother in her son's eyes, or more so."

"I am your son. I will love you forever. Nothing can ever change that or come between us."

"You will take a wife and enshrine her in your heart as you once enshrined me," Tihi said. "It is the way of things. I have known this and thought I would accept the change, but it is harder than I expected." She tenderly touched his head. "I do not like it, Son. I do not like it with all I am."

Dega had never seen his mother this way. He was troubled, but he took it for granted she would accept his interest in Evelyn and be her normal self again. "She is my friend, Mother. What harm can it do?"

"She is more than that. Whether you admit it to yourself or not, I am second in your eyes now." Bowing her head, Tihi moved off.

"What's the matter with her?" Evelyn asked.

"She not happy we fight, we run." Dega had told more lies in the past few moments than in all his life put together.

"We're not done with either," Evelyn predicted. She bent and carefully rubbed the crushed leaves into the gash. Dega winced but bore it stoically. "Now you lie here while I make some tea."

"What good that be?"

"You'll see." Evelyn had brought her mother's coffeepot. She didn't think her mother would mind since her mother and father were away in St. Louis having her father's rifle fixed. She filled it with water from the water skin and set it on the fire to heat. From her bundle she took pieces of dogwood bark and dropped them in the water. Then she went back to Dega. "It shouldn't be more than a few minutes."

"You treat me nice."

Evelyn almost said treating him nice came easy because she cared so much. Instead she said, "It's what friends are for."

Dega had more he yearned to say to her, but his tongue was oddly frozen. Coughing, he forced out, "You best friend me ever have."

"I ever had."

"Eh?"

"Your English. You wanted me to correct you, remember?"

"I sorry. I try so much, but white tongue hard." Dega averted his face in shame.

"Don't feel bad. A lot of Indians say the same. My mother speaks it so well because she has a knack for languages."

"Blue Water Woman talk good, too." Dega referred to the Flathead wife of Shakespeare McNair.

"She's had decades of practice. Marry a white girl and stick with her twenty years and I bet you'll speak English as good as Blue Water Woman."

"Which white girl?" In Dega's eyes there was only one.

"Oh, any will do," Evelyn hedged, and just knew she was blushing. "I better check on the tea." It wasn't anywhere near done, but she opened the coffeepot and looked in and put the top back on. "The tea's not boiling yet."

Over at the horses, Waku was stripping a saddle. He glanced up as his wife joined him. "Did you hear? She makes tea for us. She is a good girl, that one."

"She makes tea for our son," Tihi corrected him. "He has cast me aside in favor of her."

"What are you talking about? Degamawaku loves you as much as he ever has."

"So he says. But my spirit is troubled, husband. When we get back to King Valley and our lodge, I must think long and hard and decide whether I like the change in him."

"And if you do not?"

Tihikanima feigned an interest in the stars.

"I do not see why it bothers you so. Tell me. Would you feel the same if she was a full-blooded Shoshone?"

"I am not a bigot."

"Then let it drop. Interfere and Dega will resent it. Besides, if they are truly in love, you can never drive them apart."

"Never say never, husband," Tihikanima said, and smiled.

Chapter Fifteen

The horse he had taken from the Sioux was about done in, but Logan didn't care. He had deliberately ridden it near into the ground.

The distant glow of a campfire was why. He'd counted on Venom stopping for the night, and unless he missed his guess, the camp up ahead belonged to the bastard who shot him and the former friends who left him for dead.

Logan slowed his lathered mount and fingered the hilt of the knife. Earlier, he had come on the bodies of Rubicon and an Arapaho and out of spite cut off the black's nose. A petty act, but an impulse he couldn't resist. So what if Rubicon hadn't been with them when Venom shot him?

A few hundred yards out, Logan drew rein and slid down. He let the reins dangle and advanced on foot, staying low to the ground so there was less chance of them spotting him.

Presently Logan flattened and crawled. His former pards had camped at the base of a knoll. He counted five forms around the fire. Two were missing. The Kyler twins, he soon deduced. He reckoned that Venom had sent them on ahead, which worked in his favor.

Logan was going to kill his former boss. Here and now was as good as any other time, but he needed a gun and they weren't about to hand one to him. Staying well out in the dark, he studied on how to get one.

The five were eating. Jerky and coffee wasn't much of a meal, but it was more than Logan had. His mouth watered and his stomach growled.

No one said much. Tibbet mentioned that he wished they were eating thick venison steaks or roast buffalo and Venom growled that they couldn't risk shooting game because shots carried a long way.

Potter bit off a piece of jerky and asked with his mouth full, "Do you still think we'll catch up to them tomorrow?"

"They can't be that far ahead," Venom said. "By noon at the latest we'll have them."

"Let's hope the Kylers don't lift their hair before we get there," Tibbet remarked.

"They know better."

"What about after?" Calvert asked. "Do we keep hunting scalps hereabouts or head elsewhere?"

Venom spat. "Do you even have to ask? As soon as we're done with the girl and her friends, we're heading for Texas. There's plenty of bounty money to be made off Comanche scalps."

"I'd rather hunt them than the Apaches," Potter said. "Apaches aren't quite human."

"They pull their shirts on one sleeve at a time like the rest of us," Venom said sourly.

"That's about all we have in common. They can run all day under a hot sun without tiring, and we can't. They can go days without water, and we can't. They can kill us in a hundred different ways and do it so quietly we're dead before we know they're anywhere near."

"Don't make more out of them than there is."

Logan was watching Calvert Finally he groped himself and stood. Without saying a word, he went to heed the need.

Quickly rising into a crouch, Logan circled the camp. The sound of urine spattering the grass drew him to the spot.

Calvert had leaned his rifle against his leg and was gazing at the stars.

On cat's feet Logan came up behind him and drove his knife into Calvert's back while simultaneously clamping his other hand over Calvert's mouth.

Calvert went rigid and tried to pull free, but the long blade did its work well. Exhaling out his nose, he deflated like a punctured water skin.

Logan lowered him to the grass. He helped himself to Calvert's pistols and ammo pouch and powder horn. He hefted Calvert's rifle and grinned. He also took a large pouch Calvert always wore.

Time to kill Venom. Logan crept toward the fire. He tucked the stock to his shoulder and fixed a bead on the center of Venom's chest. Curling his thumb, he pulled back the hammer. There was a *click* but not so loud that any of them would hear. He had Venom dead to rights and he paused to savor the moment.

The pause proved costly. The firelight must have gleamed off the barrel because suddenly Venom threw himself flat, bellowing to the others as he dived. "Get down!"

Cursing, Logan fired. He rushed his shot and the lead kicked up dirt next to Venom's face instead of coring his head as Logan wanted. Whirling, Logan did the only thing he could under the circumstances; he ran.

Guns boomed. The air sizzled with death. That Logan wasn't struck he took to be a miracle. Weaving, he made it to the horse he'd taken from the Indian. Instead of climbing on, he swung it around and gave it a hard smack on the rump. Then he flung himself in the grass.

"This way!"

Dark figures went pounding past after the horse.

"He's getting away!"

As soon as the blackness swallowed them, Logan hurried to the fire. He yanked out the picket pin and scattered all the horses save Venom's with cries and slaps. More lead sought him as he galloped to the west, but his luck held.

Logan didn't expect pursuit. By the time they collected their mounts, he would be miles away.

He needed to think, to come up with a way to kill Venom and the others and have the girl to himself.

The smart thing, Logan supposed, was to forget her and light a shuck. Forget his revenge, too, but that he would never do. A man had to stand up for himself or he wasn't much of a man. Granted, by the standards of churchgoing folk he wasn't much anyway. He still had his pride.

Before too long, he would also have the white girl.

Evelyn tossed and turned and couldn't sleep no matter how she tried. Maybe that was the problem. She was trying too hard. Casting off her blanket, she rose and fed buffalo chips to the fire, then stood and stretched and yearned for the comfort of her parents' cabin.

Everyone else was asleep.

They'd debated taking turns keeping watch. As tired as they were, Evelyn had argued with Waku that rest was more important. Given that his son was hurt and his wife and daughters exhausted, Waku gave in.

Evelyn checked the coffeepot. There was some tea left. She filled her tin cup and walked a dozen feet into the dark to contemplate the stars and ponder. She needed a brainstorm. The scalp hunters would be after their hair tomorrow, and she had yet to think of a way to stop them.

Sinking down, Evelyn placed her Hawken at her side and rested her elbows on her legs. Her body was sore and weary, but her mind flew on Chinook winds. How? How? How? she asked herself.

Moccasins scraped the grass.

Evelyn glanced up and wasn't surprised at who it was. "You can't sleep, either?"

"No." Dega eased down. He didn't tell her why he couldn't sleep.

"Some hunting trip this turned out to be. We should have waited until my folks got back from St. Louis."

"My father want hunt," Dega reminded her.

"I didn't think any harm would come of it. My father and Uncle Shakespeare have done it many a time and always make it home safe. I tend to forget, I guess."

"Forget what?"

"The dangers. They make everything seem so easy. But then, they know how to do everything, so they run fewer risks." Evelyn motioned the way they had come, and when she did, her arm brushed Dega's. "If I had any brains, I'd never have gone after the two Arapahos like I did."

"You save Plenty Elk," Dega reminded her.

"Only to have him be killed later." Evelyn sadly bowed her head. "I'm doing my best, but I'm not my father. I'm not even my brother. God, how I wish he was here."

"You love him great much." Dega knew he had not spoken proper English and repressed an urge to smack his forehead in frustration.

"Of course I do. Just like you love Teni and Miki. But it's more than that. Zach is able to do something I never can. All my big talk, and I'm next to worthless."

"I confused," Dega admitted. He was touched by her sorrow and almost reached out to comfort her.

Evelyn looked at him. "All along I've been telling your pa that we have to kill the slave hunters. That it's our only chance, our only hope. But do you know what? I don't have it in me to take a life unless maybe someone is about to stick a knife into me or shoot me, and even then I'm not so sure." Evelyn balled her fists, angry at her weakness. "I'm no killer."

Dega chose his words carefully. "You make sound no kill sound bad, but it good you not take life."

"How can it be good if we lose our own because of it?"

"Good for you here." Dega touched his chest. "It mean you have peace inside. Nansusequa peace."

"Explain, if you don't mind."

Dega fought down panic. She was asking him to make clear a complicated concept in a tongue in which he was woefully inadequate. Nevertheless, for her, he tried his best. "Nansusequa like peace. Nansusequa peaceful with all people unless people try hurt Nansusequa."

"That's my own problem. I just told you."

"But not problem. It what Manitoa want."

"The spirit in all things that your people believe in? How does that enter into it?"

Dega gestured, and his arm brushed hers. "Manitoa in all life. Manitoa in you. Manitoa in me. Manitoa in buffalo. Manitoa in grass, in trees, in sky. Manitoa in scalp hunters. You . . ." He sought the right white word. ". . . savvy?"

"Yes, I get that much."

"Life special to my people. We hurt life, we hurt Manitoa. So we try live in peace with all there is so not hurt Manitoa. Savvy that?"

"It's very commendable."

"But you see?" Dega made bold to put his hand on her arm. "You commendable. You not want hurt life, not want hurt Manitoa. You have peace in heart. Nansusequa heart."

Evelyn smiled. "Thank you for the compliment. A lot of my people don't see it that way. They say we have to kill our enemies. Whole countries go to war and take great pride in the killing they do."

Dega gently squeezed her arm. "They not you. You like Nansusequa. You, what is word? You cherish life."

"I try." Evelyn impulsively leaned over and kissed him on the cheek. "Thank you for trying to cheer me. You're about the sweetest man I've ever met."

A warm tingle spread through Dega. "Thank you," he said, oddly hoarse. "You sweetest girl." He started to kiss her cheek as she had kissed his but caught himself. The Nansusequa believed that a man and woman should not kiss until after the two joined hearts in a formal ceremony, as his father and mother had done.

Evelyn saw him lean toward her and sensed what he was about to do. Her pulse quickened. When he stopped, she thought he must be shy. So she figured she would peck him on the cheek again to show him he had nothing to be embarrassed about.

At that instant Dega decided that if it was the white custom to kiss cheeks, he should respect the custom and kiss her. He turned his head slightly just as her face rose to meet his.

Their lips met.

A lightning bolt seemed to cleave Evelyn's body. She jerked back in shock and raised her fingers to her lips. "Oh."

Dega thought his body was on fire. He trembled slightly, and felt his insides roil. "I sorry," he blurted, afraid he had offended her. "I not mean kiss mouth."

"It's all right," Evelyn said softly.

"It is?"

"I liked it."

"You did?" Dega had broken out in a sweat and his tongue felt as thick as his wrist.

Evelyn leaned in close again. "You're the first boy I've ever kissed. Did you know that?"

Dega wanted to respond, but his thick tongue refused to move.

"A girl's not supposed to admit she likes a boy kissing her. If I'm being too forward, say so."

Dega wondered how she could say she was going forward when she was sitting. "I like kiss, too."

"Well."

"Well," Dega echoed, unsure what else he should say.

"Would you like to do it again?"

"I like do it whole life."

Evelyn smiled. "That's getting a little ahead of ourselves. Maybe we should take it one kiss at a time."

Dega's breath nearly caught in his throat as he asked, "I kiss you one time more?"

"You can kiss me ten times if you want."

The breeze stirred the grass. The fire danced and flickered. Somewhere to the north a wolf howled.

Dega's senses were swimming when after a while he drew back and let the cool night breeze caress his hot face.

"Why did you stop?"

"That ten kisses."

"Silly goose," Evelyn said, and pulled him close again.

Chapter Sixteen

Tihikanima brought her mount up next to her husband's. "Have you noticed them today? He has ridden at her side since we started."

"They are friends," Wakumassee said.

"No. Something has happened."

Waku gazed ahead at Dega and Evelyn. "You see more than there is to see."

"Open your eyes. They cannot take theirs off each other."

"Where is the harm in that?"

Tihi pursed her lips. "I sense they are closer to each other than they were before."

"Do you want my opinion?" Waku had learned it was always best to ask. She took it better.

"I always hold your views in high regard, husband. You know that."

"You are becoming obsessed. You do not think she is right for him so all you do is criticize. I say let them be. If it is meant for them to be together, nothing you do can keep them apart. If it is not meant for them to join, then they will drift apart with no need of help from you." Waku hoped that would be the end of it, but knowing his wife, he had his doubts.

He saw the object of her concern look back at them, and he smiled.

"I like your father," Evelyn said. "He's always so nice."

"All my family like you," Dega replied.

"Does that include your mother? Lately she's been sort of cold toward me. Has she said anything?"

"My mother think you fine girl."

"After last night I hope so," Evelyn replied, and had to avert her face because she was blushing again. She coughed and focused on a belt of trees. Most were cottonwoods, and cottonwoods were common along water. "There's a stream yonder, I suspect. We'll water the horses and rest a spell."

Evelyn assumed the lead. The undergrowth was thicker than she expected. She skirted a patch of raspberries and went around a log. Gurgling drew her to a ribbon of water no more than ankle deep and shoulder wide. Dismounting, she stretched. She knelt, placed her rifle beside her, cupped a hand, and drank. The others were soon doing the same, all except Tihikanima, who stayed on her horse.

Evelyn smiled at Dega, and he smiled at her. She dipped her hand a second time and was raising it to her lips when a square block of a white man came out of the vegetation on the other side of the stream and pointed a rifle at them. The hammer was pulled back. He grinned in wicked humor.

"The name is Logan, little lady. Tell your green friends to do as I say or I'll by God shoot them dead." He patted a brace of pistols at his waist to stress his point.

Dega started to reach for his bow, but the man swung the rifle toward him and he froze.

Waku had his bow slung over his shoulder. He

motioned to his daughters to stay still, then demanded, "Who are you? What do you want?"

"You speak English, redskin? Good. That makes this easier." Logan raised the rifle and took deliberate aim at Tihi. "Tell your woman to get off the horse. Make sure she understands I have no qualms about killing a woman. No qualms at all."

Waku translated. Thankfully, Tihikanima complied without balking or arguing.

"Good. Now I want all of you to shed your weapons and raise your hands in the air."

"No," Evelyn said.

"Did my ears hear right?" Logan growled. "You don't have any damn say, girl. Not if you care to go on breathing."

"You're one of them, aren't you? A scalp hunter?"

"I'm on my own. Now do as I tell you. Shuck your hardware or bleed."

"We won't."

"Evelyn?" Dega said.

Waku was as anxious as his son. "We do not want him to shoot, Evelyn. We must do as he wants."

"That's just it," Evelyn said. "He's going to kill us no matter what we do. If we all move at once, he'll only be able to shoot one of us before we put lead or an arrow into him."

"Maybe so, girl," Logan said. "But which one gets it? You? That boy you were making cow eyes at? Or maybe the kid?"

"We will put down our weapons," Waku said.

"No!" Evelyn had made up her mind. To surrender was certain death. "When I give the word, we attack him."

Logan hadn't expected this. Usually when he brandished a gun people did as he wanted. Inspiration struck, and he quickly said, "Look, girl. All I want are your horses. Give them to me and I'll go my way in peace."

"Our horses?" Evelyn said suspiciously.

"That's all. You can keep your weapons and your lives." Logan backed toward the undergrowth. "I'll give you a minute to talk it over. Then you bring the horses over to this side one by one." He paused meaningfully. "Try to run off and I'll shoot you from the saddle." With that, he whirled and darted into cover before anyone could think to shoot or loose an arrow.

Evelyn snatched up her Hawken and rose. Of the many perils her father had warned her about when she was growing up, foremost among them was the danger of being stranded afoot in the wilderness. "Get on your horses and fan the breeze," she whispered.

"He will shoot one of us," Waku said. "It is better we give our horses."

"On foot we'll be easier to catch and scalp."

"Him not say he scalp man," Dega pointed out.

Evelyn's every instinct was against turning their horses over. Waku, though, had already taken hold of his mount's reins. "Please listen to me."

"I not want my family hurt." Waku crossed with his animal, left it on the other bank, and came back. To his loved ones he said in their own tongue, "Do as I have done. We will let him think we are timid."

Dega went next. He was almost to the water when Evelyn barred his way and gripped his wrist.

"Not you, too. Without our horses we don't stand a prayer. We can't turn them over."

"Father say must." Dega tried to move, but she wouldn't let go. "Him wise, Evelyn. Trust him."

"Think, Dega. Why does this Logan want our mounts? What purpose does it serve? On foot we're easy pickings."

"Trust father." Dega lowered his voice so only she heard. "Trust me, too. I always do what good for you."

"Oh, Dega," Evelyn said forlornly, certain they were making the worst mistake they could. She let go, though, and after Dega came back she angrily led the mare over. Waku had gathered up Tihi's and the girls' animals and passed her coming the other way. He smiled and winked, but Evelyn didn't feel like smiling.

Logan came out of concealment, the rifle to his shoulder. "You did real good. One more thing and I'll be on my way." He nodded at the mare's saddle. "Take that rope and tie these critters in a string."

"Just so you do not shoot," Waku entreated.

"Oh, don't worry about me." Logan chuckled. "It's Venom and his bunch you have to worry about."

"Who?"

"The men who are after you. They'll catch you easy now. It'll be you or them. Do me a favor and kill as many of the sons of bitches as you can."

Evelyn overheard, and was appalled. "That's why you're taking our horses? So your friends can wipe us out?"

"They're not my friends, girl, and never were. Whether they wipe you out or you wipe them out, it's all the same to me."

"I get it," Evelyn said. "You finish off whoever is left and have the scalps all to yourself."

"Who said anything about scalps? All I want out of this is a couple of hours with you."

"Me?" Evelyn exclaimed. "Whatever for?" The leer

he gave her was adequate answer. "Lay so much as a finger on me and I swear . . ."

"You think you have me figured, but you don't." Logan turned as Waku went from animal to animal. "Hurry it up, green pants. The twins will be along directly and I need to be long gone."

"The twins?" Waku repeated.

"You'll meet them soon enough. I passed their camp about the middle of the night." Logan glanced through the trees to the east. "They think they're so damn clever, those two, but I slipped by without them knowing."

Waku made a loop and slipped it over his wife's horse. "This is the last one. Take the horses and go."

Logan wagged his rifle. "First, you cross back over. No tricks now, you hear?"

Evelyn boiled with frustration. She had to stand there and do nothing as the man called Logan took hold of the lead rope, and still covering them with his rifle, backed into the woods, taking their horses with him. "We're going to regret this," she lamented as the foliage closed around him.

Dega bounded to his bow and scooped it up. "Now, Father?" he asked in their tongue.

"Now, Son."

Wheeling, Dega vaulted the stream and melted into the vegetation, his buckskins blending in so well that he seemed part of the greenery.

"Where is he going?" Evelyn asked in sudden alarm.

"To bring back our horses." Waku left unsaid what his son must do to accomplish that.

"You had no intention of letting that man take them, did you?" Evelyn realized. "You were playing along so he wouldn't shoot any of your family."

"What else?" Waku rejoined.

Evelyn felt like a fool. She retrieved her Hawken and turned toward the stream.

"Stay!" Waku urged. "We need you to help us."

"But Dega," Evelyn said, torn between her newly admitted feelings for him, and the father's appeal.

Waku picked up his bow. "Maybe that man was right. Maybe the bad men come soon."

Hooves thudded across the stream. Logan was leaving and taking their horses.

Evelyn took another step, compelled by her heart to rush to help Dega.

"Please stay!" Waku entreated her.

Emotion tore at Evelyn like red-hot claws. "You don't understand," she said quietly. "If anything happens to him . . ."

"He is a good warrior. He will do what he must." Waku faced his wife and daughters. "Miki," he said, and pointed at a tall tree. "Climb as high as you can. Tell me what you see to the east."

"Yes, Father," his youngest daughter replied.

The girl was agile as could be and in no time was perched on a branch with one arm wrapped around the bole and her other hand over her eyes to ward off the sun's glare. "I see riders, Father," she called down. "White men."

"How many?"

"Six."

"How far?"

"As far as a bow can shoot an arrow three times," Miki reported. "Wait. They have stopped. Now they are talking. They check their guns and put their hands on their knives."

"Come down." Waku beckoned to Evelyn and translated. He ended with something he remembered Nate King saying once. "We have our backs to the wall. We cannot run."

Evelyn swallowed. She had hoped to avoid a clash. Now, thanks to Logan, bloodshed was inevitable. "How do you want to do this?"

"We hide. When the scalp men come close, we attack them before they attack us."

"Whites call that root hog or die," Evelyn absently remarked. She was thinking of Dega, of last night, of the danger he was in.

"We root hogs," Waku declared, and pointed at the flintlocks tucked under her belt. "Will you share with Tihi and Teni?"

Evelyn had no objection to giving each a pistol. She demonstrated how to hold one, with Waku again translating. "This is how you pull the hammer back," she said, and did so with her thumb. "This is how you aim. Hold the pistol as steady as you can and stroke the trigger smoothly. Don't jerk it or the pistol will kick and you'll miss."

Mother and daughter were intent listeners.

Evelyn emphasized, "A pistol is only accurate at short range. We must let them get close. When we can see the whites of their eyes, that's when we'll shoot."

Tihikanima hefted the heavy weapon and said to Waku, "I would rather have a bow, husband. Why don't you take this and I will use yours."

"I am the better archer." Waku slid an arrow from his quiver and notched it to his bowstring. He flexed the string a few times, then said in English to Evelyn, "We thank you. You are a good friend."

Evelyn gazed across the stream. "I wish . . ." But she did not say what it was she yearned for.

Waku followed her gaze. "Do not fear. Degamawaku will be back. He is a good fighter."

"God, I hope you're right."

Little Miki raised an arm to the east and excitedly cried, "Look! I can see them through the trees. They are off their horses and come on foot."

"It is time to kill," Wakumassee said.

Evelyn King felt a stab of panic. "Oh God."

Chapter Seventeen

Chapter Seventeen

Dega glided through the dense growth with an ease born of experience. He had been raised in the thick woodlands east of the Mississippi. The forest was his home. Whether lowland, prairie or mountain, he was as much a part of it as the trees and the brush and the animals he shared it with.

Dega made no more noise than the breeze as he wound among the boles. He moved low to the ground so his enemy wouldn't spot him before he spotted his enemy. The man called Logan must not get away with their horses. His father was counting on him. He would not let Waku down, would not let his mother or his sisters or Evelyn, fair Evelyn, down.

At the thought of her, Dega tingled. Last night had been the best night of his life. To think they had kissed. To think she cared for him as much as he cared for her.

Dega stopped in his tracks. Now was not the time for daydreaming. Not during a stalk. Not when he soon might need to do that which his people only did as a last resort.

The People of the Forest never spilled blood for the spilling's sake. They held life in too high esteem, *all* life, from a salamander's to a bear's, from a butterfly's to a wren's. Life was the gift of That Which Was In All Things, the Manitoa, a gift to be cherished, not destroyed.

There came moments, though, moments like this one, when in order to preserve life, a Nansusequa might have to take it.

Of late, Dega had taken to wondering if his people would still be alive if they had been less fond of peace and more fond of war. The Sioux and the Blackfeet were both warlike people, and the whites didn't dare try to take their land. Maybe if the Nansusequa had been more willing to go to war, they would still exist.

The clomp of hooves brought Dega out of himself. With a growl of annoyance he plunged through the greenery toward the source. He spied Logan on a horse, pulling on the lead rope to the others. Bursting into the open, Dega drew the arrow to his cheek and sighted on the white man's torso.

"Stop or die."

Logan whipped around and began to raise his rifle but froze and cursed. "Damn you, Injun. You've got no more sense than a slug."

"Get down," Dega directed.

"I don't have time for this. Even if you stick that in me I'll get off a shot and we'll both be dead, and for what?"

"Get down."

"Venom and his friends will be here any minute. You should be with your family and that girl."

Dega took another step and aimed at a point just below the sternum, where the shaft would penetrate to the heart. "I not say again. You no take horses. Drop rifle and get down."

Logan was mad at being taken off guard. By an Apache or a Sioux he could understand. By a smooth-faced boy who if he were white would barely be old enough to shave was an insult. He lowered his rifle stock-first, then slowly swung his leg over the saddle and slid to the ground, his hands in front of him to make the boy think he was as meek as a kitten. "There. Happy now?"

"We go back. You walk front of me with horses."

Logan had expected the boy to tell him to drop his pistols, too. The mistake would cost him. "Whatever you say, boy."

"I man, not boy," Dega said indignantly. "I Nansusequa warrior."

Logan had the lead rope in one hand and the reins in the other. He turned as if to retrace his steps. "The Nansusequa? That's your tribe? Never heard of them. Where are you from, anyhow? Not from these parts, I'd wager." Logan was stalling. All it would take was a moment's lapse on the so-called warrior's part, and he could gain the upper hand.

"We from east of great river," Dega answered.

"I could guess that much. Where exactly?" Logan tugged on the rope and the reins. The arrow's barbed tip moved as he moved. He had to pass his would-be captor.

"Ever hear New Albion?"

"Isn't that a town somewhere? Indiana or Illinois or one of those states? You're a long way from home."

"All my people die. Mountains home now."

"You don't say." Logan looked away so the boy wouldn't suspect, and then, on his very next step, he darted around his mount and drew both flintlocks.

Dega did the only thing he could think of; he spun and ran. He braced for a searing pain in his back but no shots boomed. Veering to avoid an oak, he spotted a thicket and without hesitation dived in, holding the bow at his side so it wouldn't become entangled. He went several steps, and crouched.

"You're as dumb as a stump, boy."

Dega peered through the interwoven limbs and leaves. He hadn't moved fast enough. The white man was at the thicket, both guns leveled.

"Not that you'll live long enough for it to do you any good, but here's some advice. Never talk when you should kill. Never let yourself be distracted. Now come on out with your hands empty and I might let you live a bit."

"No."

"To call you a jackass is an insult to jackasses. Either get out here or have holes blown in you."

Dega eased onto his hands and knees. "I must come this way," he lied. "It hard to stand."

"Crawl if it'll make you happy, just so you get your stupid self out here." Logan backed off. "Make like a rabbit."

"I crawl not hop." Dega moved slowly. His left arm brushed his hip—and his knife sheath.

"A briar patch, for God's sake. Didn't you say most of your tribe is dead? No wonder. Stupid makes for early graves." Logan laughed.

"Much stupid," Dega said.

"You call yourself a warrior, boy, but you're not. You're a boy playing at being a man." Logan wagged the pistols. "When you get out of there, stand up and keep your hands where I can see them."

"I will," Dega lied. He came to the end of the thicket and unfurled, his head hung low, as if he had given up hope. He turned slightly so he was sideways to Logan and the pistols.

"This was too easy." Logan laughed again.

Dega struck. He whipped his knife out and sprang, stabbing at the other's throat. The boom of a flintlock and pain in his side were simultaneous. Then he and the white man were on the ground, struggling fiercely, with death hanging in the balance.

Venom was puzzled. His quarry wasn't behaving as most quarry did. It made no sense for them to stop in the belt of trees yonder when they should be fleeing pell-mell for their lives. He didn't like it. He suspected a trick. "You're sure they're in there?" He had used his spyglass and not seen anyone.

Jeph and Seph Kyler were on either side of him. "We wouldn't say it if it wasn't so," the former declared.

"We're not liars," said the other.

Venom had his men dismount. They were out of rifle range. Only the white girl had guns. She was the one they had to worry about, if they worried at all. After tangling with Apaches and Comanches, going up against a puny girl would be like stomping an infant. "Spread out and move in. Remember I want the white girl alive. Anyone who harms her answers to me."

"And the redskins in green?" Potter asked.

"Need you ask? We're after their hair."

Tibbet coughed. "What about the Injun women? You're not fixing to deprive us of our fun, are you?"

"Drag them off and have your way. Just don't damage the scalps." Venom advanced. When he dropped flat and snaked forward on his belly, so did the others. The trees loomed closer.

Venom didn't intend to lose another man as he'd lost Rubicon. He was going to outwit the little bitch and her friends, and to that end, as soon as he came within earshot of the trees, he stood, cradled his rifle, and put a smile on his face. "I know you're in there, girl. My name is Venom. How about you and me pa-laver?"

Evelyn had him in her sights. She'd expected the scalp men to charge to the attack. Panic had set in when they went to ground. She had never been in a situation like this; she didn't know what was best to do. Now here was the head scalp hunter, saying he wanted to talk. It must be a ruse. Maybe, she told herself, she could use it to her advantage. "Go away, Mr. Venom. We don't want to have to kill you."

"Ahhh." Venom stared at the spot the voice came from. "Show yourself, girl. Neither me nor my men will shoot. You have my word."

Evelyn stayed on her belly behind a log. "I wasn't born yesterday," she responded.

"It's good you're cautious," Venom said, and went on smiling. "All I want is to find out what happened to one of my men. We came across him a ways back. We're buffalo hunters, you see. He was my best tracker and . . ."

"You're what?" Evelyn asked in surprise.

"Buffalo hunters." Venom's lie hadn't worked with the freight train captain, but he figured the girl was bound to be more gullible.

"That's not what I was told. I heard that you're scalp men, that you lift hair for bounty money."

Venom feigned shock. "Wherever did you hear such a bald-faced lie? I've got more decency in me than that. No, girl. We're buff hunters and only buff hunters."

"Plenty Elk said different."

"Who? You don't mean that Arapaho buck we found buried with Rubicon? Hellfire, he fed you a pack of lies and you believed him." Venom chuckled in as friendly a fashion as he could manage.

"Suppose you explain your side," Evelyn said skeptically.

"There's not much to tell. A war party jumped me and my men. We fought them off and a couple of bucks escaped. I sent Rubicon after them. He killed one and was about to kill the other when you and your friends came along. He didn't know what to do so he came and told me. I sent him to follow you and make sure the Arapaho didn't lead you and your friends into a trap." Venom was pleased with his lie. He told it so well, *he* almost believed it.

Confusion swamped Evelyn. She tried to remember if Rubicon ever admitted to being a scalp hunter. "I saw the warrior your tracker killed. He had been scalped."

"That's normal out here, girl. Injuns scalp us. We scalp them. It doesn't make us scalp hunters. Rubicon took it as a trophy, is all."

Evelyn refused to believe him. "What about Mr. Logan? Where does he fit into the scheme of things?"

"You've seen him?" Venom thought fast, wondering how much, if anything, Logan had told her. "I booted him from the outfit a few days ago. Caught him trying to steal from one of my other men. He's nothing but a thief. He even stole a horse."

Evelyn bit her lower lip, uncertain what to do. Everything the man said was plausible. "You want me to believe that you came after us to help us?"

"We came to see if you were safe. You being a white girl and all, we were worried."

"I'm perfectly safe, thank you. So you can go find those buffalo you claim to be after."

Venom raised his voice. "You heard the little lady, boys. Show yourselves. Let's leave her and her friends be." He grinned as his men all stood and gave him questioning looks. "Mount up," he commanded. "I'll be right with you."

They turned and made for the horses, Potter scratching his head and muttering.

"There!" Venom said to the girl. "We'll be on our way. Now do I get to see you? It's the least you can do after I went to so much trouble."

Evelyn reluctantly rose. She kept her rifle trained on him and said, "I still don't know whether to take you at your word."

"It's smart not to be too trusting."

The man was acting so friendly that Evelyn felt embarrassed. "I'm sorry. I just can't take the chance."

"Don't worry. There's no hard feelings on my part." Venom went to leave. "Say. I don't suppose you'd care to tell me your name?"

"Evelyn King."

Venom touched his hat brim. "Pleased to meet you. What are you doing out here in the middle of nowhere, anyhow?"

"Hunting buffalo, like you."

"You don't say? If you want, when we find a herd I'll send one of my men to let you know."

"We'll manage on our own, thank you."

"I understand," Venom said with feigned politeness. "Well, my men are waiting. It was nice to meet you." He touched his hat again and strolled off, whistling.

Evelyn watched them ride away with mixed feelings. Part of her still didn't trust them and another part thought she was being silly. "Oh well." She shifted the Hawken to the crook of her elbow and called out, "You can come out. I guess they weren't scalp hunters, after all."

Waku and his family emerged from their hiding places.

"You think he spoke truth?" Waku asked.

Evelyn shrugged. "I'm the first to admit I'm not much good at judging people. He seemed nice enough but you never know."

"Do you want your pistols back?"

"Tihi and Teni can hold on to them for a while, just in case," Evelyn said. She stared at the retreating figures, relieved no blood had been spilled. Then she stiffened. "Wait. Where's Dega? Shouldn't he have been back by now?"

As if in answer, a shriek pierced the air from the direction Dega had gone.

Chapter Eighteen

Degamawaku fought with all his strength. He had hold of the white man's wrist to keep the man from clubbing him while at same time he sought to bury his knife. The man called Logan had hold of his wrist, and locked together, they rolled this way and that, each straining to their utmost.

"Damn you, boy!" Logan hissed through clenched teeth. "I am going to bust your skull wide-open."

Dega stayed silent. He concentrated on sinking his knife, and nothing else. They rolled again, and suddenly he was on top. Bunching his shoulder muscles, he thrust down. The razor tip of his blade dipped toward Logan's heaving chest. Logan swore, and bucked, and Dega was almost thrown off. Grimly, Dega exerted all the strength in his sinews.

"Nothing is going to stop me, boy," Logan hissed. "Not a snip like you, that's for sure. That girl will be mine, you hear?"

A chill ran down Dega's spine. The man intended to hurt Evelyn. Newfound fury pulsed through him and his body became as iron. The tip lowered another fraction and pricked Logan's shirt.

"Not by no boy!" Logan snarled, and drove his knees up and in.

Pain exploded through Dega. Sudden weakness caused him to sag. He tried to keep Logan pinned under him, but a blow slammed into his ribs and another low in the stomach. Next he knew, he was flung through the air and landed hard on his back. The knife was wrested from his grasp. He felt a sting on his neck, and blinked. Logan had the knife to his throat.

"Any last words?"

Dega swallowed. He tensed to grab the man's wrist even though he felt as weak as a newborn fawn.

"The girl was right, you know. I figure to circle around and see who is left after the shooting is done. It should be easy for me to pick them off and have her to myself."

"You bad man."

Logan snorted, and nodded. "You're about to die and that's the best you can come up with? Hell, yes, most folks would call me bad. But do you know what? It's how I am. I'm just being me." He paused. "I didn't make the laws and rules about what's right and what's not. Were it up to me, there wouldn't be—" He stopped and glanced up sharply. "What the hell are you doing here?"

Dega had heard a footstep. He moved his head slightly to see, and was astounded. "Miki! Go back!"

Mikikawaku stood a lance length away, her hands behind her back. "I came to see if you were all right."

"What did she say?" Logan snapped.

"She worried for me," Dega translated, horrified at her blunder. To Miki he said, "Go to Father and Mother! Run!"

"I will not leave you." Miki took a step. "Father

and Mother are with Evelyn. Evelyn is talking to the white men. I was to stay behind a tree, but I had to do something."

"What did she say now?" Logan demanded.

Again Dega translated.

"Venom is here? Damn. I've got to light a shuck before he spots me." Logan drew back slightly.

Miki took another step. She said to Dega, "I saw you fighting this man. I care for you very much. I do not want you dead."

"Please, Miki," Dega pleaded.

"Can you move? How hurt are you?"

Logan still had the knife to Dega's throat. "Tell her to shut the hell up and come a little closer." He leered as he said it.

"Please go! You must not let this man get his hands on you."

"Be ready," Miki said. Smiling sweetly, she took one more step. "This is for you, white man." Her clenched hands came from behind her back and she threw dirt straight in his face.

Instinctively, Logan recoiled and swatted at his eyes.

Dega lunged. He grabbed the white man's wrist with both hands and started to scramble to his knees.

Logan tried to pull free, jerking with all his might.

It was hard to say who was more surprised when the blade sliced up and in, between Logan's ribs.

"No!"

Letting go, Dega rose and stepped back. Miki came and wrapped an arm around his waist. "You were very brave."

"He will die now, won't he?"

Logan was looking down at himself in disbelief.

Bright blood flowed from the wound, soaking his shirt. He gripped the hilt and lurched upright. Tottering, he glared at them, and his other hand came up holding a pistol. "That little snot and her dirt." He thumbed back the hammer.

Dega stepped between them and pushed Miki behind him. "I not let you harm her."

"Fine." Logan pointed the flintlock at Dega and steadied his arm. "I'll kill you first and then do her." Sweat glistened on his face and he trembled.

"You did this to you," Dega said.

A guttural sound was torn from Logan's throat. "I've never wanted to kill anyone as much as I do you, boy." He smirked, and scarlet ran from the corners of his mouth. "Oh God."

Miki tried to slip from behind Dega, but he held her so she couldn't.

Logan staggered. More blood seeped from his mouth and now from his nose. Tilting back his head, he raised his eyes to the heavens and let out a shriek. His eyelids fluttered, his arms dropped, and he keeled onto his face in the dirt.

Dega went over and nudged him with a toe. He rolled the body over and yanked out the knife. Wiping the blade on the man's shirt, he stood and slid the knife into his sheath. "I not like kill," he said to himself.

"What was that?" Miki asked.

A shout preceded the crash of underbrush. Dega spun and whipped out his knife, then relaxed when he saw who it was. "Evelyn!"

Evelyn's heart had been in her throat. She'd been afraid she would be too late. When she burst from the undergrowth and saw Dega alive and Logan down, tears moistened her eyes. She forgot herself, and threw herself into Dega's arms. "You're all right!"

Startled by her display, Dega grew warm about the neck and face. "You all right, too."

More crackling and crashing, and Waku and Tihi and Teni arrived. Both Waku and Tihi stopped short at the sight of Dega and Evelyn embracing.

Dega motioned at Logan. "Him try kill me. I kill him."

"You did what you had to," Evelyn said. "You should be proud of yourself."

Dega did not feel proud. To the Nansusequa, when they took the life of anything, be it human, animal or plant, they diminished all life.

Evelyn suddenly became conscious that she had her arms around him and his were around her. She quickly stepped back and smiled at his parents. Waku smiled in return. Tihi gave her a look that reminded her of the glacier on the high peak in King Valley. "All's well that ends well, as my uncle Shakespeare would say. That man Venom and his friends left, and Logan is no more."

"To kill is never good," Waku said. He had been the peace chief of the Nansusequa for a reason; he believed in living in harmony with all beings more than he believed anything.

"I could use some coffee," Evelyn said to change the subject. "How about some of you?"

"I need bury Logan," Dega said.

"First we should take our horses back and picket them," Evelyn advised. Above all else, they mustn't become stranded afoot. Her father had ingrained into her it was almost certain death.

Waku agreed. He took the lead rope while Dega brought the dead man's animal.

Evelyn hummed as she walked. She was delighted beyond measure that Dega was unharmed. Everyone else acted subdued. She decided a fresh batch of coffee might perk their spirits, and put a pot on to perk.

Dega squatted across from her and stared somberly into the fire but didn't say anything.

"You shouldn't be so hard on yourself," Evelyn commented.

"Father right," Dega said. "It never good kill."

"You did what you had to." Evelyn sought to reassure him. "I'm very proud of you."

"You are?"

Waku and Tihi took a seat on a log. Miki rummaged in a bag and brought out a Nansusequa flute, which she began softly playing.

Evelyn leaned back and smiled. All she had to do was get them back to King Valley safe and sound and all would be right with the world.

The next moment shadows separated from the trees. A ring of filthy, unkempt, smirking shapes, their rifles leveled, converged.

Venom's smirk was the widest of all. He strolled up to Evelyn and said mockingly, "Fancy meeting you again."

Evelyn had started to reach for her Hawken but stopped when Venom's rifle muzzle was trained on her. Intuition told her he wouldn't hesitate to squeeze the trigger if she forced him.

The Nansusequa were stunned. Waku started to rise and a rifle was brandished in his face.

Miki turned to stone with the flute still between her lips.

Dega stared at the white men in anger. The cruel stamp of their features reminded him of the white men who destroyed his people.

"Cat got your tongue, girl?" Venom taunted.

"You came back."

"God, you're dumb." Venom chuckled and motioned at his men. "Permit me to introduce my fellow hair-lifters. You're going to get to know them all before we're through with you." He did so, grinning viciously the while, playing with her as a cat played with a mouse.

The truth had burst on Evelyn with the force of a keg of black powder. "Everything you told me was a lie."

"I wouldn't know the truth if it bit me on the ass."

"You really are scalp hunters."

"Afraid so." Venom chuckled, then hauled off and slapped her so hard that she was knocked onto her side. "That's for the trouble you've given me, you little bitch. You cost me my best tracker."

"Evelyn! No!" Dega surged to his feet to help her. He only took a step when Tibbet flicked out a foot and tripped him. As he went to rise, a rifle stock swept down on the back of his head.

Waku jumped up and was given a brutal blow to the temple that felled him in a heap.

Miki began crying.

"Taking their hair will be easy as pie," Venom said smugly to Evelyn. "But don't you worry about yours. It's not your hair we want." He gestured lewdly, and laughed.

"Lord help me," Evelyn said, her hand pressed to her stinging cheek.

Venom laughed, then bent and grabbed the front of her buckskin shirt. "Have you ever been with a man, girl? You're going to be. I get you first and then the rest."

"You're insane."

"No," said a deep booming voice from out of the trees. "He's evil, child. As despicable as they come."

Venom spun. So did his men. They had not quite

turned when rifles thundered, eight or nine booming at once, and the heads of the scalp hunters burst like so many overripe melons. Potter's forehead erupted in a geyser of bone and blood. The back of Tibbet's skull exploded outward. Both twins got their rifles up, but each lost part of his face before he could shoot.

Venom was shot in the mouth. Tottering back, blood and bits of teeth dribbling over his lower lip, he dropped his rifle and uttered a manic cry. He fell to his knees and looked up just as the men in the cottonwoods emerged. His eyes widened. "You!" the scarlet ruin gurgled.

Evelyn beheld a wall of a man with a square face and stout legs and a brown short-brimmed hat. She saw him draw a pistol and cock it and touch the muzzle to the middle of Venom's forehead. She didn't look away. The blast dissolved much of Venom's brow and he oozed to the ground and quaked as if cold. Then he was still. "My word," she marveled.

The big man wedged the pistol under his belt, smiled warmly at her, and held out a calloused hand. "You are welcome for the rescue, young lady."

"Who . . . ? How . . . ? Where . . . ?" Evelyn couldn't seem to collect her thoughts.

"The name is Jeremiah Blunt. I'm the captain of a freight train bound for Bent's Fort."

His men were checking the bodies and attending to Dega and Waku.

"How is it you saved us, Mr. Blunt?"

Blunt poked Venom with a boot. "These vermin made the mistake of paying my wagons a visit. While they were there, one of them made the further mistake of mentioning they were after a white girl." He reached down and helped her to stand.

"You followed them on that alone?"

"Do unto others, young lady. I have a daughter of my own." Blunt gestured at the littered forms. "You only had to look at them to realize they were vile. For them to be after a white girl meant they had to be up to no good. So I trailed them to find out."

Evelyn impulsively gave him a hug. "We're more grateful than we can say. My parents will want to thank you."

"No need," Blunt declared. "By the way, I don't believe I caught your name."

Evelyn introduced herself.

"Well, Ms. King, you and your friends are welcome to come along with us to Bent's Fort. There's safety in numbers, and you will be decently treated. What do you say?"

Evelyn King smiled. From Bent's Fort it was only a ten-day ride to home. "I say yes."

Author's Note

I have been asked if the Jeremiah Blunt mentioned in Nate King's journal is the same Jeremiah Blunt who for many years was involved in the freight trade in the Southwest.

The answer is yes.

Blunt was a remarkable man. A devout Christian, he treated the Indians fairly and was even held in respect by the Comanches.

He was involved in several escapades that drew notice, foremost among them, perhaps, his rescue of Evelyn King.

Reports have it that an eastern newspaper caught wind of the story and sent a reporter to interview Blunt. Blunt told the man that good deeds should be done in secret, and when the reporter still insisted on writing an account, Blunt held him upside down by his ankles until the reporter promised that the newspaper wouldn't write a word.

His story continues in *Wilderness #62 : Tears of God*, available in December.

Want to get the latest scoop on WILDERNESS and all other books by David Thompson?

Join his fan club's e-mail list at:
http://groups.yahoo.com/group/drobbins.

Or check out the blog at:
www.davidrobbinsfanclub.blogspot.com.

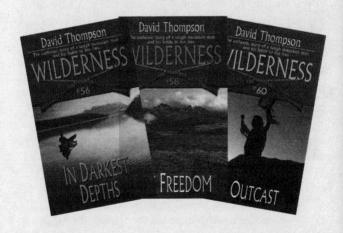

BARJACK AND THE UNWELCOME GHOST

Marshal Barjack likes to keep peace and quiet in the tiny town of Asininity. It's better for business at the Hooch House, the saloon that Barjack owns. But peace and quiet got mighty hard to come by once Harm Cody came to town. Cody's made a lot of enemies over the years and some of them are hot on his trail, aiming to kill him—including a Cherokee named Miller and a pretty little sharpshooter named Polly Pistol. And when the Asininity bank gets robbed, well, now Cody has a whole new bunch of enemies . . . including Barjack.

Robert J. Conley

ISBN 13: 978-0-8439-6225-3

The Classic Film Collection

The Searchers by Alan LeMay

Hailed as one of the greatest American films, *The Searchers,* directed by John Ford and starring John Wayne, has had a direct influence on the works of Martin Scorsese, Steven Spielberg, and many others. Its gorgeous cinematic scope and deeply nuanced characters have proven timeless. And now available for the first time in decades is the powerful novel that inspired this iconic movie.

Destry Rides Again by Max Brand

Made in 1939, the Golden Year of Hollywood, *Destry Rides Again* helped launch Jimmy Stewart's career and made Marlene Dietrich an American icon. Now available for the first time in decades is the novel that inspired this much-loved movie.

The Man from Laramie by T. T. Flynn

In its original publication, *The Man from Laramie* had more than half a million copies in print. Shortly thereafter, it became one of the most recognized of the Anthony Mann/ Jimmy Stewart collaborations, known for darker films with morally complex characters. Now the novel upon which this classic movie was based is once again available—for the first time in more than fifty years.

The Unforgiven by Alan LeMay

In this epic American novel, which served as the basis for the classic film directed by John Huston and starring Burt Lancaster and Audrey Hepburn, a family is torn apart when an old enemy starts a vicious rumor that sets the range aflame. Don't miss the powerful novel that inspired the film the *Motion Picture Herald* calls "an absorbing and compelling drama of epic proportions."

✂ ☐ **YES!**

Sign me up for the Leisure Western Book Club and send my FREE BOOKS! If I choose to stay in the club, I will pay only $14.00* each month, a savings of $9.96!

NAME: _____

ADDRESS: _____

TELEPHONE: _____

EMAIL: _____

☐ I want to pay by credit card.

☐ **VISA**   ☐ **MasterCard.**   ☐ DISCOVER

ACCOUNT #: _____

EXPIRATION DATE: _____

SIGNATURE: _____

Mail this page along with $2.00 shipping and handling to:
Leisure Western Book Club
PO Box 6640
Wayne, PA 19087
Or fax (must include credit card information) to:
610-995-9274
You can also sign up online at **www.dorchesterpub.com**.
*Plus $2.00 for shipping. Offer open to residents of the U.S. and Canada only.
Canadian residents please call 1-800-481-9191 for pricing information.
If under 18, a parent or guardian must sign. Terms, prices and conditions subject to change. Subscription subject to acceptance. Dorchester Publishing reserves the right to reject any order or cancel any subscription.